DRAWING TOGETHER

Peter Cleverly

DRAWING TOGETHER

with illustrations by

Jack Penton

and the Author

First published in 1995
by Bookhouse Publishing
Debenham, Suffolk.

Printed by The Lavenham Press,
Lavenham, Suffolk.

ISBN 0 9527355 0 4

The characters and situations in this book are
entirely imaginary and bear no relation to any
real person or actual happening.

Contents

This book is for:-

Mag, Sarah, Nick, Hugh, Richard, Paul and Keith.

We were drawing together.

Chapter One

"Arch. ass. reqd. Busy country practice."

"I've always had a very good feeling about this one," said my wife cheerfully, scanning for the one hundredth time this laconic advertisement, "A really good feeling! I think this is going to be the big one!"

"But do you *want* to go and live in the country? Even if this comes off...? Which I bet it won't!"

"Live in the country? Of course I do! Everybody wants to live in the country... have chickens and ducks and runner beans..."

"Runner beans? I wouldn't know one end of a runner bean from the other."

"Doesn't matter. Runner beans are fully reversible. And anyway, just think – you could join the local Morris Dance group, sing in the choir even. And you probably wouldn't have a cold if you'd been breathing healthy, unpolluted air. No – the thought of living in the country has a lot going for it. I could join the Women's Sewing Circle, make chutney for the Church fête... Of course we never thought of it before but when you get down to it, you begin to see the advantages so – give it your best shot, Jack."

She looked at me critically. "And, anyway, whatever else, you look very nice – sincere, hard working, yet with a certain je ne sais quoi suggesting a caring personality."

"Oh, yeah?"

"Yeah! Absolutely! All those things. So, get out there! Cleaned your teeth? Zipped your fly? Pocket flaps out? Tissues? Here, take mine. How is your cold, by the way?"

"Better," I lied, "I think it's better."

"Well, remember to blow your nose before you go in. And straighten your tie. Don't seem too keen and don't accept a penny under sixteen thousand; try for eighteen."

"Yes," I said, "Ok, I will."

"Well off you go. You look fine. Really. I'd give you a job like anything."

Off I went. The North Circular and the M25. The A12 to East Anglia, the Chelmsford by-pass and off to the left through Sudbury. Colourwashed, steep-roofed farms streamed by like so many beached Noah's Arks. Here and there, it is true, a waggon wheel, a carriage lamp or two and even a wheelbarrow full of last season's bedding plants rusting away in the frost, but in the main refreshingly unevolved. Mighty church towers presided over crowded villages or stood alone in peaceful dignity among the winter fields under a peerless blue sky, crackling with frost. From within their delicate frame of flushwork the leaded clerestory windows gave back the winter sun in gold and crimson.

My car heater purred on in the distracting way it had and under its dessicating influence my cold got steadily worse as I drew into the ancient Suffolk market town of Lavenham (pop. 1,710) and my destination.

Rank upon rank of timber-framed houses greeted me. Some were spick and span and over-restored, some pretty dilapidated still; all, to my hostile eye, were painfully self-satisfied and aware of their Grade 1 Listed status. Even on this icy February weekday the town had its share of tourists. The few shops that were not selling antiques, byegones, curios or gifts were tea shops. I eyed the place with considerable disfavour and wondered whether I wanted the job I had come so far to apply for. My disgruntlement was fuelled by the realisation that I was half an hour early. Too early just to appear. Not early enough to put a bit of custom in the way of Pam's Pantry – 'Coffee and Teas and Light Luncheons Home Made Cakes and Jams a Speciality'. Early enough to freeze to death waiting. I had come to see Sir Hastings Munro FSA, ARA, FRIBA, in reply to his brief advertisement for Architectural Assistance. I knew little of him beyond his qualifications which were good, his address (Spring House, Swan Street, Lavenham) which was impressive, his typewriter which had a chipped lower case t, his epistolary style which was laconic, his signature which was illegible and his letter head (Black Trajan Roman lettering on paper so thick that one sheet bulged the envelope into a cylinder and of which two sheets would have had to go parcel post).

Spring House, when I found it, though, was a delight.

"When Royal Anne became our Queen,
The Church of England's glory, Another face of things was seen
And I became a Tory."

And I would have become a Tory too, if it had led me to the possession of a house like that. Never was brickwork again to be so finely jointed and so rosy. Never again glazing bars so white and so satisfyingly stout, brick arches so neat or a doorcase so robust, so idiosyncratic and so welcoming. This one, within its Doric order and beneath its solid pediment contained an ogive fanlight traversed by tracery of fantastic and careless ingenuity. A flight of four steps on either side of which a wrought iron handrail reduced by age and two hundred and fifty years of wear to ribbon slenderness followed the line of the curtail step. A skirt of cobbles divided the house from the pavement and, debating first whether to drive through a side arch into a stable yard with, dimly seen, a range of timber framed outbuildings, I parked my car on the cobbles, lit a cigarette, straightened my tie, cleared my throat with an unpleasant hawking sound and settled to wait. I decided I could be fifteen minutes early for my ten thirty appointment; indeed, to have waited any longer would have exposed me to the grave risk, in that implacable frost, of hypothermia.

At the side of the door was the sort of spring-loaded bell pull that so seldom works and, fearing to break its slender and rusted wire, I gave it a tentative tweak, listening carefully for an answering tinkle within. No tinkle. A brass lion's head eyed me derisively and I seized the ring in its mouth and banged on the door. The problem with knockers is that you can either bang too gently and then be faced with the embarrassing question of when to bang again or too lustily and lay yourself open to the charge of being brash, peremptory, boorish and demanding. My knock was undoubtedly in the second class. It woke the echoes up and down the street. It rattled the window panes. The echoes had not died away when the door was opened by a sandy, terrier-like lady in fur boots, gold rimmed spectacles and a head scarf. She eyed me with surprise. She did not take the cigarette from her mouth before saying in tones of disbelief, "Mr. Alexander?"

I said no. I added, as was indeed the case, that I was Mr. Simpson, Jack Simpson.

"Your appointment is for 10.30," she said reprovingly. I agreed. I added that I was a quarter of an hour early.

"Mr. Alexander was due at 10.00," she said accusingly.

"Mr. Alexander must tell his own tale," I said. "Perhaps for the moment enough to note that he is a quarter of an hour late." I followed her into a stone-flagged hall in which, in the charming manner of the period, slate slips were set diamond-wise between the flags. "I had heard the bell," she said. "Wait in here."

'In here' was the dining room and, if the street was cold, and the hall colder, the dining room defied description. I huddled my anorak about my shoulders and paced the room to keep the blood flowing. Fine room though! A beautiful room and full of beautiful things. A set, if I mistook not, of Hepplewhite chairs surrounded the long table. Over the chimney piece were two pop-eyed children of Hanoverian aspect and a white woolly dog with unnaturally glittering eyes. No surprise to me to read the signature Zoffany. Two of the watercolours which filled the panel spaces were by Girtin and two – fine architectural pieces – by John Dobson. I estimated the cost of the contents at £300,000 till my eye was caught by the blind marble gaze of an almost chinless young man on a basalt pedestal. I read the signature Nollekens; I jacked my estimate up to £350,000.

"Don't be too meek," had said my wife. Huh! How could a man not be meek in the midst of this casual splendour? My nerves, tautened to breaking point by the cold, twanged in desperation. I fished out a calming Gauloise and lit it, took two hasty and soothing draws but then realised that the room was without an ashtray. Perhaps Sir Hastings disapproved of smoking? The curtains were, I believe, an early American print, so no wonder. I threw my cigarette at the chimney piece where a fire was laid and resumed my restless pacing to be interrupted by a noise. A friendly noise. Of all the noises so far heard in that house the most welcoming – the crackle of a newly lit fire. I was hardly able to absorb the horror of my situation (what sort of cad comes into a fellow's house and without a by-your-leave lights the damn fire dammit?) when the door opened.

Sir Hastings entered rubbing his hands and smiling cheerfully if absently round the room, seeming to check its contents with an innocent but knowing blue eye. He was about 5'6" (or 1.676 metres as we say in the business) and as nearly egg shaped as it is possible to be. His hair was sparse but stood cheerfully upwards in a tuft that made him look like Tintin. His many chins were supported by a spotted bow tie and a watch chain girdled the waistcoat of his pepper and salt tweed suit which had a surprising number of small pockets. The suit and the watch chain were of a piece and, quite consciously, built up a deliberate impression of cosy and archaic elegance.

"Ah," he said, "Alexander. Good to see you. Glad to see you've made yourself at home. But, all the same, it's warmer upstairs so come along. Don't usually light a fire in here. Chimney's not quite safe you know. But there's another chap due in a moment – at least he can enjoy it."

He led the way up the firm solidity of the staircase, glacially illumined by a round headed window on the half landing, to a panelled and bay windowed room overlooking the street. A leather covered writing table was just visible under a pile of papers and rolls of drawings. A complete set of the Shotter Boys' aquatints of London hung round the walls and another of Mr. Nolleken's best stood in the broken pediment of an immense bookcase.

The terrier lady entered with a tray, a massively piled and white hot coal fire radiated a generous heat through the room and I began to think the day was looking up. I couldn't, though, help calculating that the fireplace shared a chimney stack with the dining room below and wondered whether Sir Hastings might need a bit of watching.

"Sorry to keep you waiting," he said, noisily inhaling a cup of coffee. "Help yourself to coffee and have one of these little biscuits." He took two himself and resumed, "Had Sir John Ironbridge on the telephone. Going to do something about Dawsey at last. Terrible mess at present. Wyatt, you know. Good architect but," he lowered his voice confidentially as though Wyatt were in the next room, "careless. Terribly careless! Spoilt, you know. Too much work, that was his problem. Whatever you do, don't make the mistake of taking on too much. It's a temptation but it's ruined more than one good feller." I promised I wouldn't.

"Let me see, you're with my young friend Travers Hayward, I understand."

I said no, I was with the London Borough of Bow.

"Ah! Bow! Yes. That pretty little house in the High Street said to be by Soane. Stuff and nonsense! The minute I saw it I said Townsend and, of course, I'm right. And now you want to work in the country? Quite right. London's no place to bring up a young family these days. Good, good. Now, you'll like this!"

He led me to a rent table in the bay window and opened a large book, "'Pine's Royal Residences'. With the coloured plates. Of course, I had a copy uncoloured, but I was lucky enough to pick this one up at the Dunkley sale and this too – 'Vitruvius Britannicus' – silly chaps hadn't realised it was a first edition. You have a copy? Ah now," reprovingly, "every young architect should have a copy. Yes, Heather?" to the terrier lady who stood in the doorway.

"Will you speak to Lord Southwold? He's rung twice today."

"Yes, yes! Put him through. Now my dear Alexander, we must both get back to our duties, the res angusta domi, don't you know. And I'll ring you up. Yes, that'll be best. I'll ring you up."

I shook his hand and made from the room hearing his cheerful yapping voice as I went, "Tommy? Haw! Haw! Haw! Did you get home all right? And was Mildred sitting up? Haw! Haw! Haw! ....."

I returned to the dining room to pick up my anorak to find them both occupied by a man of my own age who stood, balancing delicately on the fender, warming his bum in front of the fire. He was tall and thin and dark. It was said of Rudyard Kipling that either one of his eyebrows would have done any normal man adequately for a moustache and so it was with the figure before me, and he had a pretty adequate moustache as well. He was wearing a dark blue, double breasted suit of a cut which Claire would have swooned over, then told me I couldn't afford, a white shirt and a tie of pale apricot silk. His socks, I noticed, matched his trousers exactly. My socks did not match my trousers and, as I came to think of it, did not, in fact, match each other.

"Mr. Alexander, I presume?" I said.

"Even so," said he. "Your anorak, I presume?" He handed it back to me and we eyed each other for a moment in silence.

"I have come," he said loftily, "to apply for a job with Sir Hastings Munro."

"Well, just fancy that!" I said. "Hard to imagine how he'll find his way amongst the talented line-up."

Alexander extracted a slim cigar from a leather case, delicately picked up a glowing coal in the tongs and lit it. "May the best man win," he purred.

"Oh, don't give up as easily as that," I said with a roguish smile.

He withdrew the cigar from his mouth, "Do be careful how you drive," he said. "The roads are terribly slippery." It wasn't only the roads that were slippery, but also, as I was to discover, the elegant front steps which were like glass and only by a back breaking contortion was I able to save myself from a spine shattering fall, clutching desperately at the handrail. When I had recovered, I observed a red Ferrari parked on the cobbles and wished with much passion that the ghastly little boy who lived next door had not written 'Also in white' on the back of my white Ford. Sitting in the driving seat of the Ferrari was a blonde girl in a blue ski suit. Her healthy tan spoke of Val d'Isère rather than Lavenham. Taking off her fur ear muffs, she tapped on the horn to attract my attention and lowered the window with a discreet hiss. "Can you tell me," she asked, with that particular smile which certain sections of the community reserve for the occasions when it is necessary to address a member of the lower classes, "Can you tell me how much longer Byam is likely to be?" I walked over to the car and leant a confidential elbow on the roof. Her blue eyes were as cold as the February sky. I didn't like her much.

"Byam?" I said. "Byam who? Or should I say who Byam?"

"Byam Alexander," she explained patiently. "He's in there talking to Sir Whatnot."

"I'm not acquainted," I said, "with the whole of the calling company at Sir Hastings' house. You'll have to give me a little descriptive detail."

"Well, he's tall and dark. Very good looking. He's wearing a blue suit ..."

"Ah! I think I know who you mean. Eyes rather too close together? Beaky nose? Ragged moustache? Yes, I know who you mean. I should think he might be another hour or hour and a half. Perhaps an hour and a quarter might be the best guess I could make."

"An hour and a quarter?" she said in horror. "I can't sit here freezing for an hour and a quarter! He said he'd only be ten minutes."

"No sensible girl would believe every word she heard from a man called Byam Alexander," I said. "But, I'll tell you what... if I were you I'd drive up to the head of the High Street and there on your left you'll find a place called Pam's Pantry. They do coffees, teas and light lunches, their homemade cakes and scones, to say nothing of their home made jams are widely esteemed in the locality and you could spend a warm hour or so while you're waiting for Mr. Alexander. If you got back in say, an hour and ten minutes, then you'd only have another five minutes to wait."

I could see she didn't like me much either, but she fastened on this suggestion with alacrity, let up the clutch abruptly and disappeared up the High Street with a screech.

I was well satisfied with this arrangement. I thought it unlikely that, if Sir Hastings' interviewing technique were consistent, Alexander would be more than another ten minutes and with the arrangement I had thoughtfully made, he would come out and find his car and his driver gone. He would be distracted. He would not know which way to turn. He might even be reduced to ringing up the police. He would certainly get very cold. He might even get pneumonia. He and the girl in the car, who, honesty forced me to admit, was glamorous in the extreme would probably quarrel all the way back to London. I leapt into my car, turned on my burbling heater and made my way back to the London Borough of Bow.

"Well," said my wife, "There you are. Come in. Poor thing, you look frozen. The kettle's just boiled. I'll make you a large cup of tea and I've cut you a plate of chicken sandwiches because I knew you wouldn't have had any lunch. I'm longing to hear what happened."

I noticed, sadly, that Claire had opened a bottle of wine and the table was laid with candlesticks, a sure sign that she was expecting a celebration. This was not going to be easy.

"Sit down and tell me everything from the beginning. You got there ... go on... Oh, firstly, did you remember to blow your nose?"

"No, as far as I can remember, I didn't."

"Were you meek?"

"Yes, I must say, looking back on it, I was pretty meek."

"Did you insist on £16,000 a year?"

"Well, if you can believe it, we didn't even mention the subject of salary."

"Darling, what *did* you say? You must have said *something*."

"Well, I don't think I said anything at all, except to confess that I hadn't got a copy of the 'Vitruvius Britannicus', but it didn't matter what I said because, quite obviously, the job is going to another bloke."

My wife gave me what I can only describe as an enigmatic smile.

"Why," I asked, "are you giving me an enigmatic smile?"

"What makes you think," she replied with the smile firmly in position, "that the job is going to another bloke?"

"Oh, there was this chap there... smooth... you know. In a Ferrari. Competent, polished, fitted in with the background. You don't have the remotest conception of what sort of joint Spring House, Swan Street, Lavenham is, Claire! Right out of my league. Say what you like, we Simpsons may not know much, but we know when we're beaten."

The enigmatic smile had become a good deal broader as I spoke and my wife now leaned forward and seized me by the ears, an uncomfortable habit she has in moments of elation or affection. "Listen to me, you great ape!" she said. "Half an hour ago, Sir Hambro Hoskins or whatever he is rang up to tell you that you had got the job and would you be ready to start on Monday week? I said yes." So surprised was my chicken sandwich that it turned aside and made its way into my windpipe and it was some time before I was able to reply, "Say that again! He said what?"

"He said you'd got the job and could you start Monday week."

An Awful Thought occurred to me. "Did he ... er, ask for Mr. *Simpson*?"

"Of course he did and I said I was Mrs. Simpson. Who should he have asked for?"

"Not... Alexander..?"

"No. What's the matter with you?"

"And he wants me to go Monday week? But that's absurd. We haven't even discussed a salary!"

"I have," said Claire complacently. "He offered you £16,000 and I said you couldn't come for less than £18,000 and we finally settled at £17,000. Satisfied?"

Chapter Two

"Fit Pair Unmatched Hinges."

On Monday week I made my way back to Spring House, relying this time on the doorbell to signal my arrival. The door was opened almost immediately and was opened with nightmare improbability by none other than Byam Alexander. Much as before, but this time he was wearing a grey tweed jacket, black cord trousers and a soft white roll neck pullover.

"Alexander!" I said, "For Christ's sake! What the hell are you doing here?"

"Delighted to see you too. Come in, come in! All will be revealed." He led the way to the familiar dining room, no warmer, no less elegant, no less deserted and no less hostile than before. "You had a letter," he said, "from Sir Hastings?"

I admitted that I had.

"It confirmed an offer of the job that he had made over the telephone?"

I agreed that it did.

"He offered you a salary of £17,000 a year?"

"No," I said, "He offered me a salary of £16,000 a year but I banged him up to £17,000."

"I too," said Byam.

"Let me understand this," I said. "You have this job offered to you in writing and you have accepted in writing. Is that the case? Then we have to accept the improbable fact that we have both got the job."

"I will go further than that," said Byam. "Did your letter conclude with the following paragraph? :-

'I am hoping over the next years to cut down my working hours to be able to travel and work less but more widely. Obviously, I can't say more until we know each other better, but you may regard the coming three years as a period of trial with a view to a partnership.'"

It was all too true and I acknowledged as much.

"Do you know," said Byam. "I think this Hastings is a devious old bastard, a tricky old twister whom it would be unwise to trust further than the end of the garden path."

The door opened at this point to admit the terrier lady.

"Heather," said Byam. " – I may call you Heather? I was just saying to our friend here that it appeared to me that Sir Hastings was an artful twister whom a wise man would not trust beyond the end of the garden path. How would you read that?"

It would be exaggerating to say that she smiled, but her lip certainly twitched in an unhostile way. "If you've found that out in the first five minutes, you may go far," she said. "Now I will show you to your place of work. It doesn't matter today, but you are supposed to use the side door."

"We Alexanders," proclaimed Byam, "always use the front door."

"It's funny you should say that, but we Simpsons have a similar idiosyncrasy. It doesn't pay," I added, "to be too meek."

"Tell me," said Byam as we followed fur boots and headscarf through the house, "You won the Tite prize, didn't you and the Bossom medal, and weren't you the Letherby travelling scholar? And didn't you come down from the University with a first?"

"Yes," I said, "All those things. How do you know?"

"I make it my business," he replied, "to suss out the opposition. D'you know the Catholic church in Cambridge? Designed by Dunn and Hansom. Dunn was the designer – the ideas man and Hansom the practical man of affairs. People said, "Dunn saw it handsome and Hansom saw it done." I'll be Dunn and you can be Hansom. By and large," he added, "with my looks and your brains, we might be a formidable combo."

"With your sauce," said Heather over her shoulder, "I should think we might all end up in jug!"

She led us to the back of the house, under the arched half landing of the main staircase, through a swing door covered with red baize and starred with brass headed nails and into a cavernous kitchen where a range the size of a Rolls Royce rusted in neglect under a stone arch inconveniently low and where solid brass taps dripped into a mottled sink which would have been quite large enough to wash a medium sized corpse and which was supported on two brick piers green with rising damp. A fine dresser filled the far end of the room, its matchboard backing seamed with the vertical cracking associated with wet rot.

"This is the kitchen,"said Heather. "We don't use it any more."

"I'm quite seriously glad of that," I said.

She led the way to a small doorway which I had supposed would lead to a not large cupboard and up a breakneck staircase with five kite winders at the bottom and four at the top to a landing illuminated by a roof light dimmed out by cobwebs. "The Drawing Office," she said, "is up here." She threw open a door and led the way into a long room. A very long room. A room so long that its further end was but dimly perceived. It was illuminated by three small leaded windows at long intervals and by three skylights which, in their earlier days, had been openable by cords, long disappeared. The length of the room was punctuated by a boarded shaft of doubtful but probably originally agricultural purpose.

"You were saying, I think," said Byam, "that this was the drawing office?" And, turning to me, "Remind me sometime to look out a copy of the Shops And Offices Act 1982. The plot is not strong and the prose laboured, but Sir Hastings might find some of the conclusions whimsical to say the least."

I said, "You mustn't think I'm criticising, Heather, but up till now, the drawing offices in which I have worked had a medley of equipment – tables for a start. I even knew one in which there was a chair."

"In these days," said Byam helpfully, "heating is not unknown and, such is the luxuriance of the times we live in, even a telephone."

"Carpets," I followed on, "I've even known carpets."

"Steady," said Byam, "Steady Simpson, let's not go over the top!"

Heather eyed us with considerable hostility. "The telephone," she said "is in Ron's office."

"Ron?" I asked.

"Yes, Sir Hastings' chief assistant." "Chief assistant? Are there others?"

"Well, there were, but they left."

"I really hate inquisitive people," said Byam, "and one shouldn't pry, but I think we need to know why they left. What reason could there have been?"

"You know bloody well why they left," said Heather, surprisingly, "They left because no one in their senses would work for five minutes longer than they had to in a tip like this!"

"And Ron?" I asked. "What about Ron?"

"Ron? Oh, Ron's all right! He's been with Sir Hastings for forty years. Worked with him before he left London. Runs the office really. What he doesn't know isn't worth knowing. He's all right, Ron. I said to Sir Hastings the other day – 'You're the most obstinate man in England.' He said to me – 'No, I'm not, Ron is!' Had to agree! But he's all right, Ron. See for yourself." She pushed the door open, saying as she did so, "I must get back, there's no one on the telephone."

Ron's office was absolutely delightful. It was about the size of the cabin deemed suitable for a not very senior officer on a not very large cargo vessel, the second engineer perhaps. It was, in fact, similarly furnished. Possibly twenty five per cent of its superficial floor area was occupied by a large drawing board and the remainder by shelves and files, schedules pinned to the walls, a calendar from a roofing company with some of the nudest girls I had ever seen outside reality in my life, and a neat list pinned to the wall said,

Monday

1 Tenders due Aldham.

2 Ring B.H.

3 Dentist 10.30

4 New blokes come?

Reassuringly amongst the orderly litter on his desk, there was indeed, a telephone.

Ron was small, he was bright, he was birdlike, he was pale of face. He had red hair, his moustache was red likewise and his eyes, when he pushed his spectacles onto his corrugated forehead were bright blue and enquiring. He confirmed that he had been with Sir Hastings for forty years but forty years had not been enough to expunge a cockney accent of an archaic sort nowadays no longer heard even in London.

"Well, well, well!" he said, "Lambs to the slaughter, eh? Sir H. said you was coming today but I turned round to him and I said, 'Are you sure? ' And he turned round to me and said, 'Fingers crossed!'"

Ron Steel – for such was his name – rattled on cheerfully, " You never quite know with Sir Hastings. I say to him 'You'll forget to go to your own funeral one of these days' and he turns round to me and says 'That's the last thing I'll forget!'" He laughed heartily and picked up the telephone which had been ringing for some while. "Steel'ere," he said, "What's that? Not enough clearance on the quarter space landing of the service stair? Which drawing are you looking at? H22B? Now Lennie, I want you to look in the bottom right hand corner – know your left from your right, do you? That's a good boy! You see a note there? What does it say? Well that's right Lennie. You're coming on, Lennie. Ring me if you have another problem. Struth!" he added, "People nowadays!"

"Who was that?" I asked curiously.

"Site agent." he said, "General foreman as we used to say. About ten years old, straight from school, like the rest of them these days. I turned round to him the other day and I says, 'An' if you want me to come round and change your nappies for you, you just let me know.'

Cheeky monkey! Like the rest of them, he thinks he knows it all but he'll learn! They all learn in the end. Now, what about you blokes? Sir Hastings fill you in at all? Not at all! I might have known it! Did he say he was off to America next week? Nah, I don't suppose he did. But that's what it's all about. We've been short handed since the end of the summer when Burton and Jacob turned round one fine morning and gave in their notice. I can't say I blame them! It's all right in the summer but get's a bit nippy in the winter an' I said to Sir H. 'We'll have to get somebody else,' but he didn't take a blind bit of notice. We get a bit busy and he puts the work out. 'I've got friends,' he says. But it won't do I says and I think he would have gone on in the same old way if this American lark hadn't cropped up. But that's the way it goes and here you are."

"Look, Ron, that's all very fine, and here we are indeed, but what I want to know is how did Burton (Burton was it?) and Jacob go to work? I mean, for a start, what did they sit on and, to go on, what did they draw on?"

"They brought their own stuff – drawing boards and that. I said to Sir Hastings 'It won't do,' but he said 'It'll work itself out.' But you'll have to talk to him about that." He looked at his watch. "He said he'd be back for lunch. I've got the dentist at 10.30. Shall we all have a get together just before lunch, say twelve?" His telephone began to ring again. "Steel'ere," we heard him say as we left the room.

"Here, I'll tell you what we'll do," I said. "Walk up the High Street to a place called Pam's Pantry and take on a little coffee and perhaps even a homemade scone or two.

Byam eyed me coldly. "Pam's Pantry? You think well of the establishment it would seem. A tiny financial interest in its prosperity have we? Eager to send them all the custom you can? No don't apologise! I will concede that it was neat, Simpson, neat!"

As we passed through the stable yard I indicated an aged MG. "No Ferrari today?"

"Good Lord! That wasn't mine – but thank you all the same. No, that belongs to Gentian."

"Gentian?"

"Yes, Gentian Woodruffe. Nice girl but with a father having all the charm and not a little of the appearance of a charging rhinoceros. Pity."

We walked up the High Street together in a silence that really was, I did believe, companionable. I took it on myself, as I thought befitted the holder of the Bossom memorial medal, to point out various items of architectural interest to my companion as we made our way. He acknowledged this with polite attention and we entered together into the steamy interior of Pam's Pantry.

"Tell me," he said as we sat down together, "Why did you leave the

London Borough of Bow, with its central heating, its buses, its corner shops, its pubs, doubtless a bingo saloon, saunas even and pensionable employment?"

"I left," I replied, " because there were two streets of mid Victorian houses, nothing very special, but all right, you know, in good condition, full of people. I know they were in good condition because renovating them was the first job I ever did for the Council. At the end of last year I was put to work on a proposed Leisure Centre. It involved the demolition of my two streets and about five acres besides. SAVE got hold of it. Piloti ran an article. The scheme was very hush hush. Somebody thought there had been a leak. Word got round that I was responsible. My promotion prospects suddenly seemed a little unstable so we jacked it in."

"Were you?" asked Byam.

"Was I what?"

"Responsible?"

"Well, since you ask, I have to say, yes – indirectly."

"Indirectly?"

"Well, indirectly because I supplied the information. Claire wrote the article."

"Claire?"

"Yes, my wife."

"Stout fellow!" said Byam. "And to forestall your next question which was doubtless, why did I leave Travers Hayward? It was a sad story. A jolly sad story. Good novels have been built round a central episode considerably less poignant but if we are to be colleagues (and it has been my observation that colleagues in the remoter parts of England quickly become friends) there should be no secrets between us. Mr. Hayward had a house in Park Village West. An increasingly fashionable area," he explained kindly. "He was having some alterations done which involved the installation of central heating. It was necessary for reasons too tedious to explain to fix a radiator casing early in the proceedings, a radiator casing for which there was no detail. 'Alexander,' he said, 'I want you to go round to Park Village, survey the recess, do a detail, take a taxi and hand it to the joinery department at Morrises.'

"I proceeded in accordance with his instructions. Owing to the above mentioned alterations, the central heating was off, the house was cold, but the welcome accorded by Mrs. Hayward was nothing of the sort. It was cordial, it was warm, it included two or three gins. We sat in the kitchen side by side, we turned the oven up to 200 and opened the door. It was very cosy. As often happens in such circumstances, friendship ripened with tropical suddenness and the long and short of it was that we spent the major part of a chilly afternoon in bed.

"Mr. Hayward, worrying about his detail, and getting no answer to the telephone, which I had thoughtfully taken off the hook, surprised us in what I believe is sometimes called deshabille. An unparalleled scene ensued. He couldn't – as he pointed out a number of times – believe his eyes. And what on earth did I think I was doing? I forbore to remind him that he had sent me to survey the recess.

"Well, that was the end of that. I didn't think it worth mentioning when I saw Sir Hastings that his friend and I had parted. But now, it seems to me that we must have a serious talk with Sir Hastings. Firstly in the matter of office equipment."

He took a pen from his pocket, turned one of Pam's menus inside out and began to write on the back :-

Tables (or desks)

Drawing boards

Chairs

"A telephone," I suggested.

"Yes, certainly, a telephone. Say rather two telephones, one each."

I agreed.

"Desk lamps"

"Something on the floor and perhaps a picture or two. What would you suggest?"

"A Fragonard," said Byam, "or a Boucher. There's a Lancret coming up at Sothebys next week – might suggest that."

"A bust or two by Nollekens?" I put in.

"Certainly," said Byam.

After half an hour and with the aid of another of Pam's menus, we had completed our list and, seeing that it was almost lunch time, set off to deliver an ultimatum to Sir Hastings.

He was, as we had already concluded, a tricky old bastard but took our suggestions without any demur. So out of touch was, and is, he with the realities that I truly believe it was in his mind that architectural assistants brought their own furniture with them. Certainly this was the system on which he had operated until we arrived to persuade him otherwise. The rest of the day was spent in conference with Sir Hastings and Ron Steel and Heather. Strange sort of meeting!

Sir Hastings lay back in his chair, his hands folded over his waistcoat, Heather, divested of her headscarf in acknowledgement of the lavish heat in Sir Hastings' room, perched on the edge of a chair with a note book on her knee, Ron, who did most of the talking, sitting at the rent table.

"That job at Mendlesett?" one of them would say. "Did anything ever come of that? What was that chap's name? Whittaker?" "Yes, better give him a ring." "If anyone's going over to Mendlesett, perhaps they ought to look in on the barn. Nobody's been there for months."

And, "Wasn't there a problem with the fireplace?" "Nah," said Ron, "I did 'em a detail."

And so it went on. There was a tremendous amount of work in the office, some pending, some building, some with a complete set of drawings, some with the barest set of sketches, tenders received but not checked, Building Regulation queries from the Local Authority. It seemed that there were two jobs of large size, one in Cambridge, one in Ipswich, each valued at more than a million and one other, of medium size, was about to start – phase two, we understood, of a luxurious retirement home. Yet another substantial contract, housing in a sensitive conservation area, should have been, though was not yet, on the drawing board. But, underlying it all, the saving grace of Sir Hastings' broad and sunny confidence that anything he did was always for the best and his clients were lucky to have him and Ron's matchless skill and experience.

We were to find that Ron was an ugly but efficient draughtsman. All his drawings were in pencil and he could produce them at the speed of light. He had, moreover, an iron grip on the building trade in Suffolk. He knew them all by their Christian names and had known many of their fathers. His specifications were often one liners but he gave the impression that no one would dare to give him anything other than a perfect job and so, as we were to find, it proved.

I wrote and scribbled. It would be exaggerating to say that light had dawned by the end of the day, in fact -

"A dungeon horrible, on all sides round
As one great furnace flam'd; yet from those flames
No light, but rather darkness visible
Serv'd only to discover sights of woe..."

The wonder, though, was not that there should be plentiful sights of woe but that, under the Munro doctrine of "It'll be all right – I'm a knight", and in spite of the efforts of the absconding assistants, anything should have reached a state approaching readiness. When at last Heather brought in the tea tray, Sir Hastings summed up cheerfully,

"Well, that seems to have tied everything up. Anything you want to know, ask Heather or Ron. I'm off to the States on Wednesday and I shall be with the Royal Fine Arts Commission all tomorrow."

When we had absorbed this information, Ron, consulting a diary black with entries, said wearily, "Your appointment with the Royal Fine Arts Commission is not tomorrow, it's Tuesday week."

"Then one of you fellows will have to go," said Sir Hastings, whose limited attention span had been exhausted for some while and, beginning to wave his hands and fidget – " Time you fellows got back to work? I'll leave you to deal with the whatnots."

By the whatnots we assumed, and after conference with Heather, confirmed that Sir Hastings referred to the office furnishings.

I returned to Ron's cabin with him and said after a while that I should really be making my way back to Bow.

"You can't go on driving up and down to London for ever," said Ron.

"No, that's the next thing – we must look for a house."

Ron reflected for a moment, "Number 14 Pottergate might suit you," he said. "Care to have a look before you go back? Getting a bit dark, but the electricity's on."

Number 14 Pottergate turned out to be the property of his sister. She had lived there since the war. She was indeed a war widow and, evacuated from East London with an East London school, she had stayed on as a primary school teacher in her little house in Lavenham which Ron confided she had bought in 1944 for £750 until her death. Waiting only while Ron made half a dozen succinct phone calls, we walked down through the frosty streets together to the town's edge. Here the blank wall of a Victorian mill interrupted the run of timber framed houses.

"Number 14's the only one left," said Ron. "It's just inside the Pottergate."

And it was. It occupied a tiny road frontage and it had that unusual and endearing feature, a return jetty supported, as I later saw, on a fine moulded dragon beam and, in consequence, had the charming appearance of a tiny fortress. It had obviously, in its time, been a shop and the hinged Medieval stall board still hung beneath the street side windowsill. I loved it. "What do they want?" I asked nervously.

"You could have it for £60,000," said Ron.

"Is that enough?"

"Oh, yes, I think that's fair. It's not much of a house really. It's only got one room on the ground floor, and two bedrooms, or rather one bedroom and an attic. The apples and pears are so narrow you can hardly get up them. Nowhere to park the car, though you might be able to do a deal with Fleming just round the Johnny Horner. There's a little bit of ground where you might be able to persuade him to let you park." He drew a large key from his pocket, inserted it in the ancient lock of the nail studded door, dim with limewash and creaking on its ancient hinges and we stepped into its spare, single ground floor room.

A single room with a polished pammet floor in all the colours between burnt sienna and indian red, one wall entirely occupied by an enormous fireplace and, indeed, one flank wall of the house, was entirely supported by a battered chimney stack rising through uneven offsets to a pair of octagonal chimney shafts.

"I'll have it Ron!" I said.

"Nah, you won't. Not until you've seen it all, you won't. This is the kitchen through here." The kitchen was a single storey extension stretching down one side of the garden and, in a cupboard tucked away beside the fireplace, a narrow staircase wound its way to the room above. By reason of the return jetty, this seemed large. Its leaded and mullioned window looked down the length of a narrow garden, separated, on the one hand, by a wall from Potter Lane, where perhaps the accommodating Mr. Fleming might allow me to park my car and, on the other, by a wall, from the water meadows. The bathroom was in a first floor extension which was supported on posts which formed a south facing open shelter, apparently full of logs. Ron waved an explanatory hand. "The October gale, you know. I bought a couple of trees and cut them up for her."

"I'll have it," I repeated. "I think we could get sixty for our flat, in fact I'm sure we could."

"Half a mo," said Ron, "you haven't seen the worst yet." He opened a further cupboard door and we wound our way round a solid newel which ran from the roof to the ground into a fine attic room with a floor of elm boards, any one of which would easily have covered a coffin. A little, peaked dormer window peered over the water meadows. Lumpy plaster hanging from the reinforcement remaining from the earlier thatch hung between the rough cut limewashed rafters. Wafer thin tiling battens supported a cascade of plain tiles, hanging each from its pair of oak pegs.

"Roof's not good," said Ron, poking it. "I've been saying to her – next fall of snow ... She wouldn't take a blind bit of notice." His bright blue eye was momentarily dimmed with affection as he spoke of his sister and, indeed, a quiet presence was as evident throughout as were her economical, sensible and practical minor arrangements.

"Come off it, Ron," I said." It's just what I want."

"I think," he smiled, "you'd better consult the boss. Won't she have a thing or two to say?"

"I think she'll go ill with lust at the mere idea of it," I said. "Can I bring her down at the weekend, or even tomorrow?"

"You do what you like, my dear man. It's not even on the market yet."

Claire drove down with me the following day and, as I had known she would, fell for the house with a bang. We arranged with Ron to rent it on a weekly basis till the sale went through and after an agonising and heart stopping series of delays and minor treacheries,(and come to think of it, major treacheries too), managed to sell the flat. 14 Pottergate was all that we had hoped and after the buses and bingo saloons of Bow our wilderness was Paradise enow. Byam established himself with one of his lavish supply of friends sharing a flat in Cambridge. Sir Hastings trotted off to America and I settled down with the perfunctory help of Byam, the solid advice of Ron and the derisive eye of Heather to cleanse the stables of Augeus.

After a month I had at least compiled a job list and had colour coded this to indicate the state of play. Blue for enquiries waiting to be dealt with, yellow for jobs requiring attention whether in the form of specification or drawing or both, red for works in hand on site , grey for contracts completed but not yet out of the defects liability period.

"Purple, perhaps," murmured Byam, "for jobs where an action for negligence is pending?"

During this same period the drawing office was furnished. It was furnished for considerably less than the £1,000 which the reluctant Sir Hastings had agreed to spend because we were to find that every firm we approached for the supply of this or the fitting of that was so anxious to do Ron, or perhaps even Sir Hastings, a favour that it was, in one or two cases, more than we could do even to extract a bill from them.

"God, or was it Matthew or Mark or one other of his speech writers knew what he was about when he said, 'To him that hath shall be given'," said Byam. "I never saw the point of that till now."

"Watch it," I said, "because whoever it was went on to say, 'From him that hath not shall be taken away even that which he hath,' and that could just be you or, worse still, me."

"Not if I know it, mate. Not if I know it!"

Chapter Three

A House Divided.

"I'm afraid Sir Hastings is in America for a few weeks, I'm putting you through to Mr. Simpson." Familiar words. I had heard them so often in various forms. To begin with Heather had said, "Shall I put you through to Mr. Simpson?" – or, alternatively, to Mr. Alexander, depending on which one of us was immediately available, but so many people had said no thank you and rung off abruptly that we had evolved this formula and found that, on the whole, it worked pretty well. Faced with my tone of level efficiency or Byam's fawning servitude, few had the heart to hurt our feelings by saying that they would prefer to await Sir Hastings' return, and so it was in this case.

A Mr. Clive Belton. He sounded self-opinionated, spoilt, rich, impatient and in a very bad temper. I was to find that he was habitually all of these things.

"Mr. Smithson? My name is Belton. Clive Belton. Your firm has been well recommended to me, though I would sooner have spoken to Sir Hastings. I've no doubt he will take the matter up on his return. I own Moat House, Medfield. I expect you know the house." I didn't. "I have to divide the house in two," he continued. "It's not a very complicated matter but the house is listed Grade two star and we need someone to draw up the plans and get the consents. I consulted the Suffolk Preservation Society and the S.P.A.B. and I had a word with old Bunny Hollister the other day – I expect you know him?" I did. He was one of the District Planning Officers from over the border and a noted bon viveur who had the reputation of giving large undertakings to his mates on the golf course, from which his wretched deputy had then to extricate him. As a consequence, he was considerably more popular with the public at large and especially the golf playing public than he was with the unfortunate planning officials. "They all mentioned Sir Hastings' name to me and that's why I've come to you. Interested? I shall want the matter dealt with quickly and I'm only normally available at weekends. Saturday morning suit you?"

Stretching the telephone to the extreme length of its flex and stretching my arm to its extreme, I had just been able during the course of this conversation, to extract Pevsner's guide to Suffolk from a distant book case and, returning to my desk, had turned up Medfield -

'Moat House. Partly of the C14, with cross wing added in the mid C15. Though much mutilated, king posts remain in the roof and the screens arches are particularly fine. Panelled door has cock's head hinges and the original sliding shutters remain on both floors in the (disused) north wing. The moat, which encloses three sides of the garden, is traversed by a three arched brick bridge of the late C17.'

While I had been gathering this information, Mr. Belton (call me Clive) had talked on describing the house in considerable, if forgettable, detail. I was able at the end to say, "Ah, yes, I know the house. Some of it must go back to the Fourteenth Century, I would think, though I suppose the cross wing might be a hundred years later. And hasn't it got a three arched Seventeenth Century bridge? It has? I thought I knew the house."

Mr. Belton was extremely impressed, "I see you know your Suffolk."

I went in to report this conversation to Ron.

"Aren't you a pair of little busy bees," he said. "Mr. A. is working on Saturday morning too, it seems."

"Never!" I exclaimed.

"Yers," said Ron. "Some old girl friend of his rang up... Hermione something... wants some alterations done and he's going out on Saturday too. Though, if I know anything about our Mr. Alexander, we've got a case of cherchez la femme. Still, I'm not complaining. Anything that can get him working on a Saturday is all to the good."

I made my way over to Medfield on Saturday and paused to view Moat House through the winter trees across its moat. It was really the best, I decided, that East Suffolk had to offer. Its steeply pitched roof was covered with an undulating coverlet of plain tiles of all colours from a red so dark that it was almost black, through buff to white, where, here and there, lime torching on the underside was showing through. I admired Mr. Belton for not having stripped and retiled it, though I foresaw, sadly, that a time would soon come when this would be necessary. Its long front was plastered and colour washed to a sort of burnt orange, dark under the eaves where protected from the rain, fading away to almost nothing at the undulating brick plinth which ran round the house. The windows were of all sorts and sizes, some leaded, others replaced in the Eighteenth Century and, for some strange reason, there were two front doors, each in an Eighteenth Century doorcase and each, in an attractive way, scaled down below the true Classical proportion in deference to the low ceilings within.

As I drove over the bridge (manifestly of the C16) a window opened and the head of Mr. Belton appeared. "Go round to the kitchen door!" he shouted peremptorily and, following his pointing arm, I did so. Architects do sometimes get shown to the Tradesmen's Entrance. I reminded myself that Mr. Belton had omitted to say and I had omitted to ask why he wanted to divide his so very distinguished house in half. I wasn't left in doubt for long.

I was received in the kitchen which was well, if not to say lavishly, equipped I guessed about ten years before. A type of standard German kitchen unit which had been popular at the time had been used, of a sort I particularly dislike, where slightly overdesigned cupboards are treated at great expense and with much ingenuity to make the oak of which they are built look as though it were moulded from plasticine. I looked about me and wondered what was odd about this kitchen until it suddenly struck me that the cupboards were completely empty and, apart from two mugs, upturned on the draining board, there did not seem to be a cup, a saucer, a plate, a knife, a fork or cooking utensil from end to end of this large room and, as I came to look, I saw that pale patches on the walls indicated places where pictures and plates, a clock and other things besides, had recently been removed. The only furniture in the room was a rather small table incongruously covered with persian blue formica and two bent steel chairs with red rexine seats.

"Sit down Mr. Simpson, and I'll explain what this is all about." He had sounded cross on the telephone. In real life, his face, it seemed, was contorted with barely controlled rage. His eyes, which were small, glowed like red hot coals and from time to time, he paused in his narrative to grind his teeth.

"My wife and I," he said without preamble, "are divorcing. We are waiting for the decree absolute, if you want to know. She and I jointly own this house and, Mr. Simpson, if you can believe this, she has insisted on retaining half the house. Not retaining half the cash value of the house, but, physically, half the house! Incredible isn't it?"

I sighed and shook my head, tut tutted a bit and he resumed,

"Incredible, absolutely incredible! Half the house! I couldn't believe it when her shyster lawyer told me what she was up to! Nothing I can do about it, legally – not morally, of course, but these lawyer chappies it seems can make the law say anything they want it to. Legally she was in her "rights". Ha! Of course, with her living in one end of the house, the rest of it is unsaleable, except at a disastrous discount, so what was I to do? I had no choice. So, after endless argy bargy, it was agreed that we should divide the house in half. I had a surveyor chap over to do an accurate drawing of the house to decide exactly what would be half. As a matter of fact, and as you'll see, it wasn't difficult to work out the division; with one half goes the office, the dining room, the drawing room and the staircase, three bedrooms and a bathroom and with the other half goes the kitchen, two bedrooms, a bathroom and the North wing."

"Disused?" I asked.

"Yes, that's right, disused, but, and here comes the incredible part – when I had gone to all this trouble and expense do you know what she said? (You're not going to believe this!) She said she wanted the South wing! Well, I wasn't going to stand for that! I mean – no one would have stood for that! 'Great God!' I said, 'When you came to me you had nothing, absolutely nothing and now you think you can walk off with half my house, with the better half of my house? Have another think, girl!' I said. Well, then, of course, the lawyers moved in. I've got nothing against my chap, but I think he was a bit wet. I said to him, 'Just stand up for my rights. Bang on the table a bit!' But you know what they're like! That's the trouble with the legal profession – they get paid as much for making a balls up of it as making a good one, so what's the incentive? Anyway, the long and short of it was we took the matter to court and the recorder said 'Spin a coin for it.' Can you believe it? The irresponsibility! What we pay these blokes for is more than I can imagine! So we tossed."

"And ..?" I asked, breathlessly.

"Well, wouldn't you know, it's all of a piece. I lost, so now I've got to make something habitable out of the kitchen, the kids' bedrooms, the North wing which hasn't been occupied for two hundred years and the spare room over which is so bloody cold that you can't put anyone in it from October until May! And her? Well she's laughing. All she's got to do is convert the office (my office!!!) into a kitchen. Drains are there, cold water's there, and she's got a three bedroomed house for which she hasn't paid a bloody penny! Makes you sick doesn't it? I'll tell you what, though. Mr. Simpson, you're a young man, I'll give you a really serious bit of advice – women! when they want something, nothing's too much trouble, but when they've got what they want – and don't you forget this – they'll turn round and cut your balls off as easy as they'd make a hair appointment!

"I said we'd call in an architect to deal with the consents and all that stuff, but what does Madam say? "Oh, no," she says, "I'm not going to use your architect! I'll employ my own." So what does she do? Goes off to some half-arsed bastard she was at Cambridge with –

practically unqualified I expect – "to protect my interests". Her interests! If you wanted to damage that girl's interests, you'd have to take a battleaxe! But I'm relying on you Mr. Simpson. I'm relying on you to deal with this "architect" of hers. The lawyers have let me down and landed me in the mess I'm in today, but when it comes to building, that's a different matter! We must take the initiative and we must hang on to it! That's why I've gone to your firm – because I don't mind what I spend. It's a matter of principle, you understand," he added.

"Now, let me show you round. This is the kitchen, or was, but I think if we cut this end off it'll make a perfectly good dining room. Through here's the store. We haven't used it except as a store but it faces East and West so it would make a perfectly good drawing room and this little lean to bit at the end will make a loo with all the gubbins. Of course, thanks to Madam next door, we are reduced to the back stairs, but there are two rooms here that the children use (that's my two by my first marriage) and if we could do something about the heating, this would make quite a good bedroom here. Nice view across the garden but there is one thing I don't want and that is to have to look out of my bedroom window and see Madam lying about in her bikini at all hours of the day so I want to build a bloody great wall to go from half way between those two windows there to just to the left of the tree down there. And if you will come and look over this side... I want the wall to go on here down past the end of the moat. I'm not having anybody else use the bridge except me so she can make a new entrance on the other side and then when her lah-di-dah friends come to call, they'll have to drive round the end of the old pig sty. Won't do them any harm.

'Well there you are Mr. Simpson, there's the brief. Think you can handle it? I want it dealt with very quickly if you please. I know that Listed Building Consent's involved, but I want this finished with and out of the way and, above all, I don't want you to have anything whatever to do with the other half of the house. I've insisted that any Specification written or any drawings prepared should be to your approval and I want you to make it tough for them! If there's a single comma missing – you tell 'em! As you've probably gathered, I'm a very reasonable man and I want no more but I insist on having no less than my rights in this matter. I've been buggered about quite enough already. I'm sure you understand my position."

I said that I totally understood his position, I was sorry he should be put to so much trouble and aggravation and that I would do all that I could to mitigate it and that he could totally rely on me to ensure that the other side got no more than a hundred pence in the pound. Did he know who the architects acting on the other side were?

"Anderson or some such name," he said vaguely and we returned downstairs to consider the, I must say excellent, drawings of the premises as existing, which had been prepared by the surveyor chap.

As we parted, he apologised for his lack of hospitality – "Can't even offer you a cup of coffee I'm afraid. Every bloody thing that was in the kitchen has gone down the other end. Can't gain access to get as much as an electric kettle back."

I had noticed, as we had inspected the upper floor, a pass door half way down the passage through which there protruded the ends of a dozen or more four inch nails driven in from the other side and I well understood his predicament.

On Monday mornings it had become our habit to have a session which I could hardly dignify with the name of staff meeting since much of our time was taken up with hearing what sort of weekend Byam had had, and much of our remaining time was so interrupted by telephone calls to Ron, that we hardly got any business done at all. The purpose of these gatherings was, however, to discuss the pending week's work and to recapitulate on the achievements (if any) of the week immediately preceding. On this occasion, miraculously, Ron's telephone remained silent, but, characteristically, Byam took the centre of the stage and opened the proceedings in reply to a question on how his meeting on Saturday had progressed.

"Poor little Hermione!" he said with unnatural seriousness. "Poor little thing! Damned sad really. I remember her so well at Cambridge. Hermione Brook-Carstairs she was in those days and everybody's favourite girl. I even had a slight tendresse for her myself, if the truth were told." Gusty sigh. "It all seems a long time ago now. And then she married this chap, ten, fifteen years older than her. Plenty in the bank but not much between the ears and bugger all between the thighs as far as I could make out. Treated her shockingly! Never at home. Planted her in this great house in the country and expected her to have everything ready when he condescended to return.

"Of course, it didn't last and I think she's been very brave, very brave indeed. And, by God she's needed to be! Had to fight every inch of the way and not a penny to fight with. The long and short of it is that they've agreed to divide the house in half and what we're instructed to do is first and last make sure that this scoundrel, who will be occupying the other half of course, doesn't put one over on her and secondly to convert a room which used to be the office into a kitchen.

"I did some sketches when I was over there. I thought perhaps we could have a sort of little breakfast area here – it faces south west and then if we had a range of units along this side we could lose the hot water cylinder in a cupboard here and on the return, it might be rather nice if we had a double sink in a slate draining board rather like the one we designed for that woman at Edwardestone and then, if the money runs to it, we might take up the floor and put down some of those slate pavings. It could be rather nice."

"Byam," I said, "tell me some more about this place.... "

"Well, it's a typical East Suffolk farmhouse, though rather a good one, listed grade two star, moated with a nice little Seventeenth Century bridge... "

"Seventeenth? I would have said Sixteenth Century."

"Sixteenth, Seventeenth, what does it matter?.. And, anyway, what do you know about it?"

"Compose yourself, my boy," I said. "Far be it from me to clobber your idyll with Hermione, but while you were patting her little hand and doubtless gazing into her tear-drenched, innocent blue eyes, to say nothing of tearing off some snappy sketches of her kitchen, I was the other side of the party wall. What we're really doing is acting for *Mr.* Belton and a very prominent part of our instructions in the matter is to make sure that the architect chappy employed by Mrs. Belton doesn't put anything over on us.

"Struth!" said Ron, "I will say this – you blokes certainly make life interesting."

"Christ Almighty!" said Byam. "What are we going to do? I can't let little Hermione down. I won't! You'll have to ring this Belton and tell him to seek elsewhere."

"No," I said, "You ring this Hermione and tell her. Look what happened with Mrs. Hayward. I can tell when you're on a collision course and we don't want anything like that, thank you very much!"

Ron cocked a speculative eye from one to the other and Byam shot me a venomous look. "I don't see why, come to think of it," he said after a pause, "we shouldn't do both. They're not on speaking terms. They won't compare notes. The firm can act for Mr. B. and I'll act for Mrs. B. Good heavens! You don't often get paid twice for the same job! And anyway, I didn't exactly spell it out to Hermione that I was working for Sir Hastings. She thinks I'm in private practice," he added, looking a little shifty.

"OK," I said resignedly, "enter the jobs as two separate jobs on the list and hand me the purple highlighter!"

I put some drawings together at intervals during the week, crammed in wherever I could find a few moments to spare from the stables of Augeus and took them over to see Clive Belton the following Saturday. I found him peering from the window. "Come here and look at this," he hissed. "Don't much like the look of him! Just the sort of gawd 'elp us she would pick up.

"Who is it?" I asked.

"Her architect if you please! With a crooked lawyer on one side and a smarty pants architect on the other, I can see we're going to have our work cut out."

I peered through the window. ("Don't let him see you looking"). And sure enough, there were Byam and Little Hermione pacing the garden together in earnest converse. Byam was waving his arms about and pointing and Hermione, I was very sorry to see, was gazing up at him in what I could only identify, even at that distance, as speechless admiration. "Stupid twit!" I thought, "Why the Hell didn't he tell me he was coming over this morning? He knew I was due here. We're going to look bloody stupid if we meet." But I needn't have worried. Clive was so eager that we shouldn't even see each other that I was constrained to stand back from the windows and lurk every time we passed one.

My scheme on the other hand was well received and I have to say it was a very good one as is so often the case when the work is done against time and in a white heat of creativity. I began to think this job might not be too bad. Clive proved to be a curiously receptive client, a good listener and obviously accustomed to making decisions. It was helpful, also, that a major part of his plan was to create for himself a house so beautiful that Little Hermione would be sick with rage and jealousy at having chosen the other end of the house.

The store, which was to be converted into a drawing room was long and low. It had seen better days, as was shown by the roll moulded main beams and the chamfered subsidiary joists, their stops decorated with a pretty little country-made acanthus. It was only awaiting a little loving care to come back into use as a fine room. Towards the end of our meeting, I took a club hammer and a bolster and chipped off a little plaster and revealed the bressemer of a noble fire place about eight feet across. Any fool would have known it was there but Clive was immensely impressed and we parted on the best of terms, I so enthusiastic that I hurried home and by Sunday evening had the drawings complete and a schedule of works on tape.

Byam, too, had had a successful meeting and we began to compete with each other as to who could get his half of the house ready to go first. He even wrote me a letter -

Dear Sir,

MOAT HOUSE, MEDFIELD.
Belton v Belton. Proposed compartmentation.

It is understood that under the terms of the settlement between Mr. Clive Belton and Mrs. Hermione Belton (hereinafter referred to as the parties) it is necessary for any works of alteration undertaken by the party of the second part should be to the approval of the party of the first part. We are accordingly attaching hereto copies of our drawings numbered 0.1 – 0.4 inclusive together with a schedule of works proposed.

We would be grateful if you would seek your client's approval to what is shown and advise.

Yours truly,

Byam Wetherby Alexander R.I.B.A.

I wrote back :-

Dear Sir,

MOAT HOUSE, MEDFIELD.

We are in receipt of your esteemed favour of the 15th instant and will make an early opportunity to seek our client's instructions re same. Assuring you of our best attention at all times,
I remain for and on behalf of Sir Hastings Munro A.R.A. F.S.A. F.R.I.B.A.

Yours most truly,

John Simpson, R.I.B.A.

And on the following Saturday I made my way once more to Moat House.

"Bloody Hell!" said Clive as he looked at the drawings. "What's all this balls? She can't afford this sort of thing! What is she using for money? Who's backing her? That's what we're going to have to find out. What's her connection with this architect chappy? That's something else I intend to find out. He was over here last week, you know, spent about four hours as far as I could tell. You mark my words, Jack, there's more in this than meets the eye! Slate draining board indeed! What's that going to cost I should like to know?"

We had thought that it would be convenient if there had been two contracts perforce but only one contractor, but in the end, we decided that this arrangement, convenient though it would have been, would inevitably and eventually blow our precarious cover which got more and more threadbare by the day. In the end, we arranged with only a little manoeuvring and cooking of the tenders that two mystified contractors should be engaged. I was by this time nearly a month ahead of Byam and it seemed just possible that I would be finished before he started, but here the contract ran into a snag.

As was necessary with a listed building, I had made an application to cover Clive's unclimbable wall dividing the garden.

"Why not a nice trellis or a pergola perhaps?" asked the Planning Officer. "Something temporary, not a bloody great wall. It'll look terrible! Ten feet high? Your client must be nuts!"

The furious rage in which Clive spent so much of his time had actually simmered down a little bit over the last weeks. The glee with which he contemplated the shock horror that would sweep over Hermione when she saw his completed house had kept him in a state bordering on euphoria. The opposition of the Planning Officer however returned him to normal.

"Bloody little squirt!" he said, "Who the Hell does he think he is? And are you sure you need Listed Building Consent to build a wall? You must have got that wrong! Just tell him next time you see him that if he wants an expensive appeal on his hands, he's going the right way about it! Tell you what. I don't imagine you need Listed Building Consent to dig a foundation underground, do you?

I said I thought you probably didn't.

"Well, then, tell them to get on and put the foundations in, then we'll push it through to appeal. If the appeal succeeds, well and good. If it doesn't, we'll build the wall when the buggers are looking the other way. Let's not waste a digger on site. Bound to save a pound or two if we only have one delivery of Readymix. Can't think why you didn't think of that yourself!" he grumbled on.

As a matter of fact, he had now and to my relief, to be away for a month and I was able to confine myself to routine visiting without the endless debates with Clive that had been so prominent a feature of the last few months.

His return was signalled by a telephone call very late one night, so late indeed, that Claire and I were in bed. She took the call. I pressed my ear to the receiver and we listened together.

"Is that Mrs. Simpson? Clive Belton here. Sorry to ring you at this hour, but I've only just got home. Is your good man available? You won't mind my saying this I know, dear, but you're married to a very clever fellow. This room of mine is looking fantastic! I expect you know all about it but you must come over and see it sometime."

Claire made the sort of deprecating noises and expressed the grateful thanks which she considered appropriate to the humble role of architect's wife and passed the telephone over to me.

"That you old boy? Just telling the Lady Wife how pleased I am with the job. It really turned out very well and, I say, old boy, I was quite right to raise the height of the mantelpiece. Have you seen it? I knew you'd agree. Now, the question is – When am I going to see you?"

Claire wiggled out of bed and ran shivering across to the dressing table and put my diary in my hand. We made a date. (Bring the wife). With further expressions of appreciation and gratitude from which an element of self-congratulation was not absent, he was about to ring off when he added, "Oh, by the way, did you give instructions for the foundations for the garden wall? You didn't? Well, you should have done, but don't worry. Leave it for the time being," and he rang off.

Next time I saw him, he was in a pensive mood, "I don't know who that architect feller that Hermione got hold of is, but he hasn't done a bad job at all, down the other end."

I was amazed. "Have you seen it?" I asked.

Clive looked a little shame-faced, "Well, I did just drop in," he said. "It's not bad, not bad at all. Makes a better kitchen than this. They've rubbed the units down with lime and given it a coat of beeswax. Looks pretty good and that slate draining board we were talking about – it only cost a hundred quid. Shows what you can do if you know where to look. No, I was quite impressed."

"Has, er, Hermione seen the new drawing room?" I asked.

Clive became even more shifty. "Well, yes, she did just glance in a couple of days ago."

"And what did she think?"

"Well, old boy, I'll tell you truly, she thought it was bloody marvellous! But there, I'll say this for Hermione, she's got a good eye, always had a good eye. She never liked this kitchen much. I thought she was just complaining because," with a return to his normal manner, "she's never happy unless she's got something to moan about. But she was quick. Yes, there's no doubt about it, she got the point of what we'd done and, of course, the insulation you put in the walls and ceiling of the big bedroom has made all the difference in the world. She was amazed! I'll say this for her, she's got a good eye! Do you know what she said ? She said, 'When we sell the house on, the next people could have the office as a dining room, keep the new kitchen down my end and turn the old kitchen into a billiard room.' I've always wanted a billiard room," he added wistfully, "Still, that's enough gossip. Now come and look at the colour samples upstairs..."

When I got back Byam had a similar tale to tell. "You haven't half got me into trouble!" he said indignantly. "Spent the whole morning with Hermione trying to explain why she couldn't make her drawing room look like your new drawing room. For the first time I began to see why that marriage broke up. She's bloody obstinate you know! Won't take no for an answer. Drive a man mad! – 'Oh, but Byam, you said...' and 'Well, how much would it cost?..' and even 'You're just being difficult...' and then, to cap everything, 'You sound just like Clive...' Me! Bloody Clive!" and with a heavy sigh, "Not much gratitude in our business." "Oh, ho," said Ron, who had been listening to this conversation when Byam had wandered off to seek a little sympathy from Heather, "The course of true love never did run smooth. I said to him, 'You can't win 'em all. Just send in an account, grab your money and run! That's the way to run an architect's practice.'"

My next meeting at Moat House was at the bleak hour of nine a.m. at Clive's special request; he was racing that day at Newmarket. Pursuant to a repeated invitation, I had, on this occasion, brought Claire with me. We found the house in silence. The doors were locked, a couple of milk bottles sat on the doorstep and the Daily Telegraph was thrust into the letter box. We wandered about for a minute or two, embarrassed, not quite knowing whether to knock or not

"The bugger!" I said, "He's forgotten!"

Perhaps he had, but at last a tousled head appeared at a bedroom window. Beaming smile. "Jack! Mrs. Simpson! What *will* you think of me? Overslept, I'm afraid. Here, let yourselves in." He threw a large bunch of keys out of the window. In a few minutes he made an appearance, looking, I thought, pretty unsavoury in a Yukata (based on a design worn by the Samurai). I was aware of scurrying footsteps in the room above. "Cherchez la femme!" I whispered to Claire as Clive poked inefficiently about among the coffee cups. But he was back before we could speculate any further.

"Come along, Mrs. Simpson, while the kettle's boiling, come and have a look what we've been doing." He led the way through to the drawing room, explaining and exclaiming as he went and taking Claire through the whole design process, how he had thought this and, though Jack had initially thought that, I had finally come round to Clive's way of thinking and didn't Claire agree that it was a great improvement?

As a matter of fact, it was an easy conversation. With the early morning sun shining through the east window, the room looked superb and, as is often the way with a recently decorated room, about twice its normal size. Claire found no difficulty in admiring and pushed the old shutters backwards and forwards in their ancient grooves which, having been rubbed and rubbed with a candle end, were running like silk, with much delight. I could just hear Clive saying "That wife of Jack Simpson's has got a good eye. She didn't waste any time getting the point."

Eventually, we went on our way, mystified. "Who was that upstairs, do you suppose?" we said to each other.

When in due course the answer came I was amazed, though I suppose, if I'd had my wits about me I could have seen which way the wind was blowing. Hermione had decided, in his words – "To give it another whirl." In Hermione's words, as later reported by Byam –

"To forgive and forget and try again."

The plain fact was, of course, that neither could bear that the other should be better housed. Clive hated the thought of Hermione swanning about amongst Byam's elegant lime-washed units and Hermione couldn't bear the thought of Clive lolling, perhaps even with 'another woman' in my oh-so-successful drawing room. The idea of being in a plus billiard room situation appealed no less strongly to Clive than did the realisation that a reconciliation would put him in a minus alimony situation.

Chapter Four

Up Tails All.

When Byam was bored he had the most irritating habit of answering the telephone in a voice not his own, though I must admit, he did this very convincingly. I was in terror that he would one day be rumbled by an important client who would rightly suppose he was being treated with less respect than he deserved. Byam had a Glasgow Scots voice, what I think was meant to be a voice from the Tyneside dock area and – probably best of all – the high sing song voice of a Hindu, though this was not always distinguishable from his Man of the Rhondda. Today he selected a glottal and seemingly shifty voice from London's East End and, with a considerable sinking of the heart, I heard him say,

"I am sorry, Mr. Alexander has got someone viv 'im. No, 'arf a mo ... I fink 'es free nah." Then, holding the telephone at extreme arm's length, "'as that bloke gorn yet? Right. Putting you through now."

I hissed at him across the table, "That's your worst yet!" but Byam had now resumed his normal voice, or indeed, an unctuously charming version of his normal voice, from which I concluded that his interlocutor was an interlocutrix.

"Alexander here," he purred. I hoped he wasn't going to add, "And how may I help you this bright a.m.?" which he did sometimes. He didn't. "Who did you say? Amanda? Yes, Amanda? What can I do? Oh, dear, I am sorry to hear that. Well, nothing occurs to me immediately but I'm sure it's something we can cope with – just leave it with me for a few minutes. Are you by a telephone for the morning? Leave it with me and I'll come back to you. No, no, no trouble at all."

"Christ!" said Byam, hanging the telephone up, "The things we get asked! Here's some mad girl who rings to tell me that the moat at Belfield Hall is choked with pond weed! Now what am I supposed to do about that? Ron!" he added as Ron came briskly into the room. "What do you know about pond weed?"

"Pond weed? It's green. They have it in ponds. Why? Who wants to know?"

"A girl called Amanda Prentice who lives at a place called Belfield Hall."

"Oh, Belfield Hall! We did a lot of work there last year. Belongs to Jake Starr, the pop singer. Amanda Prentice is his PA. Nice kid. Oh, yer, I know Belfield Hall! Full of pond weed is it? Well, tell 'em to get some ducks."

"Ron, you wouldn't be sending me up I suppose?"

"No," said Ron. "Ducks, that's the thing! They'll shift it."

"Ducks? How am I going to get hold of ducks on a Friday afternoon?" and then to me, "Look, old boy, I've got to go out in a minute, can you deal with this? I said I'd ring that sweet girl back again. See if you can organise her a few mixed ducks."

I eyed him sourly, "It's a poor architect who can't drum up a few ducks for the Personal Assistant of a leading popular singer. I would have thought this would have been just your scene."

"You'll do it so much better than me," said Byam, hurrying from the room.

As a matter of fact, the acquisition of twenty ducks proved very little problem. Of course, Ron knew a reliable supplier, a supplier indeed who was prepared to deliver the immediately following Sunday. I agreed a price. I called Amanda Prentice back. I accepted her warm thanks. I told her to expect twenty mixed ducks for lunch on Sunday.

I rang Byam that evening, suppressing as best I might the note of quiet triumph in my voice and told him that I had solved his little problem. "You musn't hesitate to come to me when you're in trouble. I like you young fellows to bring your difficulties to me."

Byam was uncharacteristically impressed by my efficiency and dispatch and, after a little general chit chat, declared his intention of going to Belfield Hall to oversee the delivery of the ducks.

"Slimy old twister," said Claire, disapprovingly, when I passed this piece of information on to her. "Sneaky toad! He wouldn't be averse to a bit of dolce vita and the high pop scene. I can just see him accepting a Bloody Mary or two from the husky Amanda and I can imagine the reluctant modesty with which he will accept an invitation to lunch."

At this period, Claire did not approve of Byam although she had never met him. "I don't like the sound of him," she said. "I don't think he's a good influence on you. I know the sort – you'll do all the work and he'll get the credit." And, I must say, in support of this view she got a good deal of mileage out of the duck incident.

When I came into the office on Monday I expected to find Byam full of traveller's tales of the jolly good lunch he'd had, of the glittering company and the ease with which he had secured his return invitation. Not so. He was gloomy, morose and preoccupied. "You and your ruddy ducks!" he said.

"Why? What's the problem? Didn't they turn up?"

"Yes they turned up, all twenty of them. They were in very good form. They made a good impression. They had plenty to say for themselves. Mister Starr and his assembled guests were delighted. He thanked me warmly, 'Don't thank me,' I said modestly. 'You should thank my PA, Mr. Simpson.'"

"I bet you didn't!" I said.

"Well perhaps I didn't quite say that," said Byam. "But I did say that you would deal with a little problem which arose."

"Oh, yes?"

"Well, as I was saying, Mr. Starr was overjoyed with the ducks. He thought they were perhaps the best thing he'd ever bought (and that for a man who owns two Lamborghinis is saying a lot) and the only thing that was worrying him is where the ducks would sleep. I explained that the ducks were accustomed to sleep on the bank, often standing on one leg with their head under their wing."

"I'm sure that's flamingoes," I said.

"Well, ducks or flamingoes, it doesn't matter very much. Mr. Starr at least was prepared to accept my information at its face value. Then I was foolish enough to say that they would sleep quite happily on the bank unless a fox came along in which case he might find he was a few short in the morning. He was astounded; he was horrified; he whitened under his tan; he pictured the scene in all its horrible clarity. He wrung his hands, a thing I've never seen anybody do before. 'What,' he asked, 'is to be done?' And this is where you come in."

"I come in? I'm not sure about that!"

"Oh, yes, definitely where you come in, because I said that what he needed was a terrace for the ducks to sit on at night time on the far side of the moat so that ravening foxes would pace up and down, slavering and howling to the tune of derisive laughter from the assembled ducks on their security terrace. It shouldn't be a very complicated drawing – I doubt if it will take you more than a morning. I doubt if it will take you as much as a morning."

"Well, I'll tell you here and now that I'm ruddy well not going to do it! You're going to do it. It was your dotty idea."

"But I'm not good at terraces," said Byam. "Ask anybody – they'll all say the same – 'Excellent architect, Alexander, but not to be trusted with a terrace.'"

"You only need a little practice," I said. "Now get on with it!"

It was very difficult to get Byam onto the drawing board. He would do anything to avoid it. He paced the room, he told a number of stories, he went off and had a chat with Heather and another chat with Ron, he strolled up the High Street and had a cup of coffee and it wasn't until about noon when he got back to the office that he put a piece of paper on his drawing board, sharpened a pencil and went to work. By about two o'clock in the afternoon he was waist deep in paper and by about four o'clock an elegant contrivance was beginning to appear. It had thrown off, I noticed, a wrought iron gate in the Gothic manner. I looked over his shoulder.

"You can't do that!" I said . "It'll cost thousands!"

"I think it will cost three thousand," he said complacently. "That's one hundred and fifty pounds per duck. Cheap really!"

I left him to it. When I came in the next morning Byam's scheme was finished, much as I had seen it the night before, save that the moat's edge was decorated with a line of little iron bollards connected by a swinging chain and I mentally put the estimate up to about four thousand. Pinned to the drawing was a note to say 'Gone to Belfield to sell the attached to the Meistersinger'. I wrote 'You're quacking mad!' at the bottom of this and put it on his drawing board.

In the middle of the afternoon he returned in a state of great elation. "Never," he said, "have I witnessed a scene of such unbridled enthusiasm! He went for it. They all went for it. Amanda," he added "thought it was wonderful. And so it is!"

Some weeks later Byam's duck terrace (with its little run of iron bollards and its Gothic gate) was duly completed and duly admired. As it was immediately under the kitchen window and enjoyed a south aspect, the ducks thought very highly of it too. I went over to see it myself. I wondered whether Byam had bothered to get Listed Buildings Consent.

As I stood admiring the weed-free, clear water of the moat and the elegant line of the Duck Walk a slender figure who could be none other than Mr. Starr himself came strolling round the corner. I introduced myself as Byam's PA. He was enthusiastic and was congratulating himself warmly on having had the idea, "That should keep them safe!" he said. By this time I was rather fed up with Byam and his duck terrace and the urbane Mr. Starr who had four thousand pounds to spend on it. I decided to introduce a note of disquiet.

"I am not quite sure, though, what happens if there is a hard frost and the moat freezes over? Foxes would come from far and near and gallop across the ice like that awful scene at the beginning of Dr. Zhivago. The ducks will be defenceless; they will be backed up against the wall." I'm not sure that I didn't go on to draw a parallel between the carnage which would ensue and the massacre at

Cawnpore in the Indian Mutiny. Mr. Starr was much dismayed and was disposed to blame Byam for not having thought of a hazard so obvious. He wrung his hands and waved them in the air. He had the reputation of being prone to sudden bursts of petulant rage and for a moment it seemed I was to be privileged to witness one. I did my best to divert his mind.

"How would it be," I said, "if a series of little duck houses were built along the back of the terrace and," – warming to my theme – "each could be fitted with a vertically sliding door. These might operate on some form of trip mechanism through a set of solenoids, animated in their turn, by a frost thermostat that would come on when the temperature reached, say, three below."

Mr. Starr was pretty impressed by this and when I had sketched a series of little classical pavilions of duck size on the back of an envelope, he became positively lyrical and we parted with expressions of esteem.

When I got back to the office, I was greeted by Ron in a high state of glee, "I dunno what you said to our Mr. Starr when you were over at Belfield Hall, but Mr. A.'s had him on the phone for an hour. Twinkle Twinkle is off to Australia at the end of the month and there was something about six classical pavilions with frost-operated, guillotine doors? Got to be finished before he goes!" Ron laughed heartily. "I should keep out of Mr. Alexander's way if I were you! He'll have your guts for garters!"

Indeed, Byam did not join in the general mirth, though Heather did, "Christ," she said, "You and your bloody ducks! Why don't you think before you say these things? And anyway, what's a sodenoid?"

"Now, now," said Ron, "ladies present! Don't want any of that sort of talk, thank you very much" and, laughing no less merrily, he returned to his cabin.

As a matter of fact, with his customary skill, Byam extricated himself from the problem. The man with whom he shared a flat in Cambridge was a member of a college which had recently invested in four peacocks. After six months or so of bitter warfare on the subject, in which the Senior Common Room had been split from top to bottom into pro-peacocks and anti-peacocks, the anti-peacock faction had won and the word had gone out that the peacocks must go, if anyone who lived in the first court was ever going to sleep again. Byam had agreed to take them and, with a truly Renaissance gesture, presented them to Mr. Starr. "No Gentleman's residence complete, you know, without peacocks," he had told him.

Twinkle Twinkle was overjoyed by this Medician largesse and the peacocks became his pride and joy. And since, diet wise, they were even more fox-friendly than the beleaguered ducks, his anxieties were easily diverted and the few remaining weeks before his departure to Australia were occupied with the perfunctory design of fox-proof roosting perches in the manner of Chippendale in his Chinese period. The ducks were left to shift for themselves, which they did pretty well. They multiplied exceedingly, in fact, and wild duck came from far and near to share the hospitality of the kitchen window and the comforts of the duck terrace which soon became impossibly over-crowded and about five inches deep in duck shit.

Chapter Five

The Churching of Simpson

It is a requirement of the Inspection of Churches Measure of 1955 that every Anglican church should have a structural inspection and report every five years. It is a further requirement of the same measure that such inspections should be carried out by a qualified architect. The men and women entrusted with this activity are known collectively as the Diocesan Inspecting Architects. Some are good, some are bad, most are indifferent. Sir Hastings was good but Ron was better. In fact, amongst this array of qualified but variable talent, Ron was something of an oddity.

In the days following the passage of the Architects' Registration Act 1923, those entitled to describe themselves as architects were divided into three categories – those emergent from Architectural Schools became Associates, those full of years and girt about with professional distinction – or such was the theory at least – were, as the ultimate accolade, elected Fellows. There was, however, a third category which consisted of people (men in those days) who, having no formal training of any sort, but in substitution for this years of professional experience, could, if suitably recommended by a Fellow or two, become Licentiates. It was only necessary to find a couple of biddable seniors and this qualification was theirs for the asking.

These degrading class distinctions were swept away in the 60s but some survive to wear these obsolete distinctions. Sir Hastings Munro, F.R.I.B.A. was one, Ronald Steel L.R.I.B.A. was another. Had he been ten years younger, Ron, in spite of his matchless knowledge and experience would never have been able to describe himself as an architect and the churches of Suffolk would have been poorer for it.

Luckily for them, both Sir Hastings and Ron appeared before the world as D.I.A.s , though of recent years, as far as one could discern, Ron had done all the work.

One fine Spring morning, I encountered Ron at the door of his cabin, looking like a Christmas tree save that the binoculars, cameras and thermoses with which he was draped were not gift-wrapped. The Christmas tree impression was sharpened by the fact that he was wearing an ancient and shapeless green mackintosh.

"What's your problem, Ron?" I asked. "Had enough? Thinking of defecting to the East? If so, you've left it a bit late!"

"Nah," said Ron, "Got a couple of QIs"

"QIs?"

"Quinquennial Inspections," said Ron and then, suddenly, "Care to come?"

It was a lovely day. The sun shone without and birds sang. Within, early blue bottles buzzed against the skylights. Heather's typewriter clattered incessantly and Byam, encased within his Walkman, was apparently singing along with Pavarotti. There seemed worse ways of spending the day than doing a couple of QIs with Ron. Despairing of breaking through 'Parlami d'amore Mariu' I slipped a note under Byam's elbow saying,

'Like unto the deaf adder that stoppeth its ears and heareth not the voice of the charmer, charm he never so wisely – I write to notify you that I am going ashore with Ron. Back in a fortnight.'

It had been a damned long winter and this was the first day since we'd moved to Suffolk that I had even begun to see why everyone spoke so highly of the county. The ditches after the winter rains were brimming but willows were beginning to show a haze of yellow. The ranks of poplars that had seemed so dark and miserable through the winter were dusted with green.

"The Hounds of Spring," I said to Ron,

"Are on Winter's traces.
Mother of months in meadow or plain,
Fill the hollows and windy places
With lisp of leaves and ripple of rain."

"Yers," said Ron. "We'll have a go at St. Mary's Totton first. One of my favourites. We've done a lot of work there. This'll be the fourth time I've inspected it. Four times five is twenty. Doesn't seem like twenty years! And I'll tell you a funny thing about Totton! First time I come here with Mr.H., as he was then, 'Tell you what, Steel,' he said to me, 'I'll leave you to do the tower. I'm just going to see how they're getting on at Tinningham. I'll come back and pick you up.' Course, I knew what his lark was – this was in the days of the Reverend Beverly, 'Rev Bev' we used to call him. Terrible old nuisance.

Wouldn't leave us alone. Followed us round all morning and wouldn't stop talking.

"'You don't have to wait, Beverly,' says Mr. H. but did he take the hint? Nah. I could see that Mr. H. had had enough and so he shoved off and left me to it.

'Coming up the tower with me Rev.?' I said.

'Well, no. Ha, Ha!' said Rev Bev, 'Getting a bit old for towers.'

'Well, that's something,' I thought, so I went up and done the tower. Dirty old place it was in them days. That was before we rehung the bells, of course. Poor old place, roofed in felt during the war and leakin' like a bleedin' sieve, three or four feet of pigeon shit up there so when I come down with half a pound o' bat shit down me neck I was feeling pretty pissed off to say the least. When I got down into the church, there was this old bloke, long black overcoat down to his ankles, leaning on top of the font writing something with his old black hat beside him. 'Oh, no!' I thought, 'That's all I needed! I thought the silly old geezer had gone home to his tea!' So I locked up the little tower door and turned round to give the key back to him and start again on another long jaw. But, believe you me when I got over to the font, there was no one there. I looked out through the door and there was old Rev Bev right down the other end of the lane, talking to some old biddy at the Rectory gate. Cos, you see," said Ron reflectively, "church inspections, they've been going on for years even before The Act. Six hundred years, and some old bloke thought he'd come back to keep an eye on his church. I've never forgotten it. Keeps me on me toes sometimes. Nah, I've never forgotten that old bloke." He laughed heartily, "Not like some of them nowadays – much as you can do to get them to unlock the place for you. Bust a gut writing these reports but they don't read them half the time."

We arrived at the beautiful church of Totton. I could see why it was one of Ron's favourites. It was a double aisled church with a leaded nave roof. There were nine windows in the clerestory and the flushwork panels dividing them were enriched and given a jewelled brightness by the pretty East Suffolk practice of brick voussoirs.

"Sir H. releaded the clerestory last year," said Ron. "Beautiful job! Hardly a speck of new glass and nearly all the Medieval glass back in the tracery lights. Looks a treat!"

It did. The sun was full south and threw a splash of coloured fragments at random across the pale wall of the north arcade.

"Commissioner Dowsing, grudging sod, smashed every bloody thing he could reach," said Ron with venom as though this vandal act had been committed but the week before and not in the early days of the Protectorate. "Still, he couldn't get up to the clerestory. Be thankful for small mercies. Tell you a funny thing though – a few years ago we was dealing with a church in Norfolk, doing a bit of soil lowering (you have to sometimes). We stripped the top soil off and what do you think they began to find? Fragments of stained glass, about a foot down. Sir H. reckoned one of Cromwell's heavy footed squaddies put his boot through the window and there it was still. Not all of it, of course, but what we could find, we put together again. Well we'd better get on with it I suppose!"

We stepped outside together. Noticing that Ron, for all his panoply of equipment, seemed not to have a dictaphone in his hand, I offered him mine.

"No thanks, Jack," he said waving it away, "Never use 'em," and went on surprisingly, "When I was at school, there was this girl in our street. I used to follow her about. Ever so shy I was in those days." With his diminutive stature, his bat ears and his red hair, I could well believe it. "Didn't dare say a word but I found out she went to evening classes – shorthand and typing course – so what did I do? Signed on! I was the only bloke. But after a bit we took to walking home together. That's the way to do it! If you want to get what you want in life, you have to plot and plan a bit. So I ended up doing this shorthand. That's why Sir H. took me on. I went round all the sites with him taking all his notes."

"What happened to the girl, Ron?"

"You'd better come round one evening. She'll tell you!"

He started scribbling and chatting, partly to himself, partly to me.

"Ridge tile on the chancel needs pointing but it'll go for a bit till they have to retile. Ought to secure the eaves courses though; weathering against the crossing wall doesn't look too clever either. That gutter's only been there ten years – rusting through – and why? Because the lazy sods won't paint the insides. Pointing's getting a bit sandy but it'll go for another five years. We releaded the chancel window, oh, it must have been twenty years ago. Not so clever, we could do it better today." We strolled on round the church, I half listening to Ron's muttered commentary, my whole attention engaged from time to time by his caustic asides until, working round the church ("Always go round a church clockwise – if you go round the other way, widershins, – a witch'll get you.") until we came to the south porch.

The south porch, in all its hues and textures, and all its sturdy grace had acquired through the years something of the quality of an ancient and faded tapestry. The parapet was adorned with the crowned monogram MR for Maria Regina and alternate panels were filled with exuberant geometric patterning. The original flint filling had fallen many years before and had been replaced by some long forgotten artist's hand in a dull red mortar. In conjunction with the dark blue black of the adjoining knapped flintwork, the effect was charming.

"A lot of that red fill had fallen out," said Ron. "Some clown administering the grant said to replace it in flint. 'Stuff and nonsense,' says Sir H. 'We'll put the red fill back where it's missing and I'll defy anybody to know we've been here!'

"It was a right beggar to match. You can mix the stuff up and you can slosh in a handful of this and that but you never know what colour it's going to dry. So what did we do? The blokes had a good fire going and we mixed up a sample and put it on a shovel. Baked it out over the fire until we got it spot on! Clever stuff!" He chuckled remininscently. "You have to use your loaf of bread," he said and we resumed our tour.

As we worked our way around the church to the cold and sunless north side, we came on a young man at the top of a short ladder. He was wearing skin tight jeans and trainers and a tee shirt bearing the legend 'Arriba Ibiza!' His hair was fashionably and expensively spiked and gelled and his single earring swung rhythmically with his hammer blows. A set of mason's tools was neatly laid out on the ground beside him. The minute we saw him Ron began to scold, "Darren!" he shouted,"You silly born bastard, the sun may be out but it's not that warm! Haven't you got a coat?"

The young man turned with a grin. "Got one in the van, Mr. Steel," he said.

"Well, for God's sake, put it on – use your common!" and then – "Didn't expect to find you here today."

"I'm not here. I'm really at Wyverstone but the corbel head came back yesterday and I said to Mr. Dawson, 'That's not far to Totton.'... So I came round to fix it and there she is." He leaned back away from the wall and we saw the little Gothic face that he had just reset below the label of one of the tall aisle windows. He cocked a thumb at the balancing male head on the other side of the window, "That old boy, he looks right cheerful now he's got his Missus back!" he said with satisfaction.

Ron and I went on our way with a further admonition to Darren not to catch his death of cold. "Good boy, that," said Ron.

Before we left, we stepped back into the nave. The arcades leaned outwards at a distorted angle and I was only partly reassured by the massive square Victorian tie rods.

"Is that all right?" I asked, indicating the angle of the spread with my hands.

"It'll do," said Ron. "It's buttressed by the aisles and they haven't shifted. There's a lot of cracking in the spandrils but it's covered with monitoring pins. I said to Sir H. 'You're not sowing grass seed,' but he said 'You can't have too many.' We check them every year or so. It'll do. See me out any way."

In the afternoon we made our way to the second of Ron's jobs – to the extraordinary church of Aspel St. Lambert. In 1748 this parish had been blessed or cursed, depending on how you look at it, by a notably eccentric squire. A squire who was, as we must suppose, obsessed with the art of change ringing. His passion was seriously circumscribed by the fact that his parish church and its fine square Medieval tower only contained and only had room to contain, a paltry minor ring of six bells.

With the cheerful independence of the squirearchy of the day, he tore down the top of the tower with its three foot thick walls and rebuilt it in timber, thus gaining space for a royal peal of ten bells. He lay nearby in a full periwig, resting negligently on an elbow, one fat stone hand upraised and pointing in eternal admiration at his achievement.

I was not surprised, in all the circumstances, to see that the pub by the church was called the Ten Bells and Ron and I stepped inside for half an hour or so before our assault on the structural condition of the church of St. Lambert, that most obscure of saints.

In due course, we struggled our way through the massive hanging bells, through the murmur of pigeons and the dust of 200 years while the Spring sunshine through the louvred windows marked the mighty bell cage with bars of gold.

"Watch the ladder when you open the hatch!" warned Ron. "The ladder rungs aren't too good. I had one break under me once. Frightened me to death! Dropped me torch. It fell about 20 feet and hit a bell. Sir H. was down below and do you know what he said? 'You rang, Sir?' Very comical he thought it was."

Mindful of Ron's warning, I braced my feet as far apart as I could on the rungs of the ladder and lifted the massive hatch which must have been covered with ten pound lead.

"Mind how you put it back," said Ron "when we come down. Get your fingers caught in that, and you'd be here till we inspected the church in five years time."

"Very comical," I said.

As I stepped onto the roof, the rustle and murmur of pigeons was joined by a low droning sound. "God's truth!" said Ron, "Bees! Look there!" he said, pointing to a knot hole in the wooden parapet.

"No, there," I said, pointing to another.

"Here, there and bloody everywhere," said Ron.

"I'll tell you what – you're standing on the roof of the biggest ruddy bee hive in Suffolk! Dammit, they're all over the place."

And it was true. Through the knot holes and every other hole, we now saw, bees were pouring in and out of the tower. There must have been at least four nests, perhaps more – I didn't wait to investigate.

"Got a bit of a problem here," said Ron, "We're supposed to be

starting work up there next week."
"What do you do?" I asked, "Fumigate?"
"Nah," Ron shook his head with a knowing smile, "Ring the bee bloke. He'll come round one fine night and take 'em. I'll ring him tomorrow. It's early in the year – he won't be too busy yet."

Ron duly rang the bee bloke and, by so doing, ushered in a minor drama. As soon as scaffolding had been erected the bee bloke arrived one night with his little van, his mask, his gloves and, I imagine, a plastic bag or two.

Armed with a torch of some power, he made his way onto the roof and, doubtless found all the bees in bed. Taking a nail bar with which, on Ron's thoughtful advice, he had equipped himself, he proceeded to dismantle the boarded linings. One may imagine him contentedly working away but he reckoned without the vigilance of Mrs. Hilda Rose in her cottage nearby, who, on her way to bed, looked out of her window, saw a van in the churchyard and a shadowy figure outlined against the torchlight on the roof and heard splintering and cracking noises as well. "Someone," she thought (reasonably enough I dare say) "is stealing the lead off the roof of the tower." And, shaking with excitement, she dialled 999 and summoned the aid of the Suffolk Constabulary.

There had been a number of lead thefts in the locality and, unusually, there were three patrol cars in the more or less immediate neighbourhood. Chatting to each other on the intercom, they concerted an encircling movement. One was to approach the church by the main gate, one was to come up the lane from Church Farm and one was to station himself by the side gate in case the miscreant, abandoning his van, attempted to escape on foot. One of the intrepid officers stationed himself at the foot of the ladder and, at an agreed signal, all turned on their headlights. The leading policeman addressed the night as follows over his loud hailer – "The church is surrounded! Come down with your hands up and no one will get hurt!"

Up till then, the bee bloke had had a satisfactory night. He had been contentedly smoking a cigarette on the roof of the tower, congratulating himself on a mission accomplished, surrounded by plastic bags full of indignant bees. He had just begun a gingerly descent with a plastic bag or two in each hand when the night was split open by headlights and an injunction to come down with his hands up. Interpreting this instruction all too literally and doubtless scared witless by this intrusion, he dropped his plastic bags which whistled to the ground and exploded with a squashy thud amongst the encircling gendarmerie.

A night long to be remembered in Aspel St. Lambert!

Chapter Six

The Flood.

"But why are we doing it, Ron?" I asked. "It's a hell of a long way away."

"It's not far really," said Ron. "Hour and a half? Two hours? And we're doing it – well – to begin with, it's listed Grade One and to go on with, Sir H. wrote this report on it five years ago, didn't he, and, to finish up with, the Chairman was a cousin or something of Lady M."

"It" was a pub in one of the Hertfordshire new towns which, judging by the photographs, hardly deserved its Grade One listing and onto which, judging by the notes, sketches, reports and so on in the file, there was to be built a large extension containing two new bars, a dining room, ten bedrooms, car parking and a garden.

"Anyway," said Ron, "I've made you an appointment for Thursday week to meet some blokes from the brewery. They say they've got a good survey, but you know what breweries are like. I should take your little tape measure and perhaps your box Brownie as well. You never know what they may have been up to since we last had a look and you may find the photographs a bit out of date."

On Thursday week as instructed, I set off for the new town of Stevendon, an hour and a half or two hours away. On the back seat lay a pad, three pencils (one H, one HB and one 3B), a tape, a measuring stick and my Nikon F4 alongside a yellow hard hat and a donkey jacket with Wimpey written across the back, lent to me one bitter afternoon two or three years before and which had become so valuable that I had somehow forgotten to return it.

So parochial had we become, with no job in the office more than an hour away, that a journey of two hours seemed quite a formidable undertaking, but I was glad of it and glad also that Ron and I, warmly supported by Heather, had firmly set our faces against the eloquent case made by Byam for car phones – those brutal invaders of the only private space left in a busy world.

I arrived at Stevendon, brooding on the philosophy of new towns (or satellite towns as they were formerly called) and remembering that their declared purpose was to cure London's problem of overcrowding and thinking that successful, or at least tolerable, in themselves, how dismally they had failed in their primary function. I wondered, as I often did, where all the people came from. With half a dozen or more large new towns built round London and with every house of any size in London divided into flats, it was still necessary for the indigenous inhabitants of London to move further and further out and travel further and further in.

Thus philosophising, I found myself almost unawares in the middle of Stevendon and driving down Gainsborough Drive, off which, as I had been told, I would see a road to the left called Turner Lane which would lead me to my destination, the only listed building in the town, "The Prince Of Wales".

I began to look about me, but too late, because I became hideously lost. Gainsborough Drive led to Reynolds Terrace, Reynolds Terrace to Constable Way, Constable Way turned into a cul de sac called Romney Close. Backing out of Romney Close, I tried my luck down Lely Drive. Lely Drive only led me back to Constable Way. In despair, I began to wonder if I should have been told to turn right and, on this premise, glancing anxiously, for by now I was fairly late, down Whistler Walk, Turner Lane presented itself to me. At last, and thankfully, I negotiated this and found, buried in about a quarter of an acre of untouched Hertfordshire, a very shabby and seemingly uninteresting whitewashed and steeply slate-roofed little pub from which, on a not well designed wrought iron bracket, a fanciful representation of The Black Prince announced my destination.

A Mercedes Coupé was parked on the gravel amongst the squalid débris of beer crates that seems to accumulate around the back door of every pub in the country and from this there uncoiled a tall figure.

I am, as a rule, a neurotic punctualist and am more accustomed to sitting for half an hour in the car checking my files than arriving, as on this occasion, in a fluster of apology and ten minutes late. Simon Melford, the brewer I had come to meet, grinned good naturedly back and shook my hand. He was, to my considerable surprise, somewhat younger than I. He was, as I was shortly to discover, born in the brewery purple and owed his place at so young an age on the board to his ancestry; but only in the first instance because I was quickly to learn that, despite his romantic appearance, and languid manner, he was efficient, decisive and imaginative and, when the occasion demanded it, quite surprisingly bloody-minded.

He cut short my apologies, "Don't tell me – You got lost amongst the artists! Gainsborough Terrace and all that. We've got another pub down the other end of the town which is among the authors and by the time I've unravelled Dickens Avenue from Thackeray Walk and Trollope Approach, I'm usually late too. Never mind – Come in and I'll show you round."

The Prince Of Wales was very small indeed. It was little more than what used to be called a Beer House. I really couldn't imagine why it was listed at all and had not the remotest guess as to why it could have been listed Grade One. I put this question to Simon.

"Ah, yes..." he said, "Grade One listing. Damn nuisance. It's because it's built on crutches."

"Crutches?"

By this time we had made our way into the tiny bar and the Landlord joined in the conversation, "Not crutches!" he said "Not crutches, Mr. Simon, CRUCKS! That's why it's listed Grade One, because it's 'cruck built' and there are only two others like it in the county. That makes it very early."

As he spoke, and without any prompting from either of us, he had pulled two pints and handed one to each. They had that sort of earthy honey taste characteristic of English bitter at its best and my opinion of Melfords rose accordingly.

"Bring your drink with you," said Derek Laker (Licensed to sell beers, wines, spirits and tobacco, for consumption on or off the premises) "and I'll show you." He led us up a small staircase into a tent-like bedroom and proudly displayed the enormous crucks on which the original and clearly very early house depended. They stood at intervals down the length of the house dividing each minute bedroom from its neighbour like so many giant wishbones, wishbones that might have come from the skeleton of the fabulous Roc.

"Sir Hastings' idea was that, whatever we did, the little house should be put back to its original form so these things can be seen," said Simon. "It seemed like a good idea to me and I said so."

Bending under each cruck in turn, we made our way down a secondary and even more precipitous staircase into the second bar.

"We don't often use this room," said Derek Laker, "except perhaps at Christmas time. It's difficult to keep it warm."

"Outlook's not very inspiring either," said Simon.

We each opened our file and sorted out Sir Hastings proposal and he put before me a practical series of comments on these, prepared by himself and the brewery surveyor. Sir Hastings' idea – in addition to the restoration of the little house – involved the demolition of the squalid range of living quarters that had been added at the back and the introduction of a new entrance from a car park to be formed. A generous service area giving onto a ground floor cellar and two bars leading in their turn to a dining room were projected. A flat for the Landlord appeared over the kitchens and a garden flowed on from the door of the dining room. A secondary entrance included a reception area and a staircase up to a bedroom floor above. I wondered if Sir Hastings had considered problems of means of escape in case of fire and decided that he hadn't and made a mental note to check the regulations with Ron.

"The scheme's all right as far as it goes," said Simon, "but we shall need an underground cellar as well. The bottle store is nothing like big enough and we shall need a family room of some sort and I thought it could be planned here with direct access to the garden."

"Barbecue area at the end," said Derek Laker, "Don't forget my barbecue area, Mr. Simon."

My mind began to work. In the extraordinary way that this happens, all parts of my brain, conscious and subconscious, went into action together and a flood of information, speculation and calculation began to tick through an internal computer which seemed to gather and correlate the evidences, pointing the shortcomings, proposing and rejecting tentative solutions, offering other solutions and, as this happened, a whole department in the mind opened and began to consider elevational implications while the structural department began to consider roof junctions and a small green voice proffered the thought that if changes were made it would be possible to save a couple of fine trees which Sir Hastings' scheme had reluctantly sacrificed.

While this process was pouring through, half my conscious mind stayed open to listen to Simon and Derek Laker. The automatic vocal department came up with the appropriate "Yeses"and "Noes" and the occasional "Maybe" or "Good idea" and even "Yes, I think that might work very well". At last I said, "Could we just go and look around outside, I've hardly seen the site yet and I don't quite understand the site boundaries – for instance, does this bit here, this bit edged in red belong to us? Could there be access from the lane? Does it link through Shephall Lane? If you extended the footpath across here all the people living down here could at least come in on foot..." My voice trailed away and then that extraordinary thing you might call inspiration came upon me.

Other architects have agreed with me that this exists. You arrive on a site. You know nothing about it. You may not even – as in this case – have met the other side. Your mind is a blank. Sometimes, in the most poisonous and embarrassing way, your mind remains a blank, but, as often as not, a voice outside yourself seems to take over. And so it was on this occasion. As we walked round I fell silent and the matter began to flow.

"How would it be..." said my voice, "if, instead of putting the two bars side by side, they were at right angles to each other. At that rate they would both face south and they would both get a decent view, especially the second bar. You could see right down the green as far as the church. The service could be here between the two, which would make deliveries for the bottle store much easier. You would need to move the whole thing over a bit, but it wouldn't be a bad idea to make more of a dégagement between the new and the old. It would solve quite a problem of roof junction if you made the entrance this shape instead of that shape. I know this is only a ditch, but it's got water in it and – didn't I see that there used to be a little pond here? Why don't we restore it?"

"Ducks and geese?" said Derek enthusiastically, "Right next door to the family room. Kids like feeding ducks – 'Can we go down the pub and feed the ducks, Mum?' – Can't you hear it? And while they're feeding the ducks, Dad will have taken a couple of pints on board without even noticing it."

"Put a little dispense bar down at the end here?" suggested Simon. "For summer use. "You'll spend the whole of the summer hosing down the paving, if I know anything about geese!" he added discouragingly." But I could see he was impressed.

We made our way back into the bar and put Sir Hastings' drawings down on the table. I put a series of sheets of tracing paper over this and, 3B pencil in hand, sketched out the alternative. It worked extraordinarily well. Problems arose as I drew but as fast as I drew, their solution arose beside them and when I was able to point out that the existing trees would neatly take their place on the edge of the paved area I almost got a round of applause.

"Well," said Simon at the end of it all, "That seems to be that. What's it all going to cost?"

I had the sense, bought by bitter experience, to make no prophecy.

"Apart from your underground cellar which won't be free, it won't cost any more than the previous scheme. In fact, it ought to cost a little bit less – only one entrance, no cross over. If the loos are down here, it shortens the drainage run by about 50 metres, always assuming that Sir Hastings has put the main sewer in the right place."

"Let me take it home and work it up a bit." In truth, so pleased was I with what I had achieved, I was eager to do exactly that and as soon as I possibly could.

"Can you remember all this?" asked Simon. "If you can, I'll take these back with me today. We've got a meeting tomorrow and I can get preliminary approval to the change. One of the problems is that Sir Hastings' scheme was only approved last week but I think I can turn them round."

He could. A cheerful telephone call the following day was to instruct me to proceed. "Draw and Proceed" I wrote on the job list and happily changed the colour coding from blue to yellow – from 'pending' to 'drawings required.'

It was late on that first day when I got home to Pottergate. I had stayed on to measure and photograph. My journey much delayed by an incessant search for laybys, since, every time I had to pass through the bar, Derek Laker – without even noticing what he was doing – I believe – pulled another pint and I was sure that, in spite of a considerable intake, I had left half a dozen half empty glasses dotted about the property and its grounds.

In spite of the many stops on the way home I reached Pottergate in extremis and banged desperately on my own front door, running on the spot while I waited for it to open.

All other preoccupation faded in astonishment when the door was opened to me by Byam.

"Oh, hello, Jack," he beamed welcomingly. "Thought I'd drop in and give you this."

'This' was my pay cheque. I was surprised and not entirely pleased to see him. I had looked forward to a cosy evening telling Claire how clever I'd been and wasn't quite sure if I wanted yet to share this with Byam. I was, moreover, and on more general grounds, very surprised to see him, for although he and Claire had, of course, met from time to time, I had not felt that they had achieved or would ever achieve anything more than a guarded neutrality. Claire can be quite puritanical at times and, I suppose my stories had done better than adequate justice to Byam's eccentricities but perhaps less than adequate justice to his good nature.

I had thought there was something odd about Byam's appearance when he opened the door and it wasn't until I was well inside the house that I realised that he was wearing an apron across the front of which was written 'Faisons l'amour, pas la vaisselle!'

"Why are you wearing my pinny?" I asked peevishly.

Claire emerged from the kitchen pink, steamy and cheerful. She handed me a glass which she filled from an already half empty bottle. "Because he's showing me how to make gratin de pommes de terre dauphinois," she said.

At a very advanced hour, and at the end of an evening when it seemed no one had stopped talking for a second, I waved Byam away from the front door to walk his way up the Pottergate to pick up his car at the office. I returned to the house to find Claire all smiles.

"Why didn't you tell me how nice he was?" (Nice!)

"Behind all that confidence, he seems quite lost somehow." (Lost! About as lost as a king cobra in a kindergarten!)

"Poor chap! He's really got nobody." (Good Lord, he's got everybody!)

"Did you know his father has cut him off completely? He never really forgave him for not going into the army. I can't imagine Byam in the army."

"I can!" (A vision of Byam in the tight blue patrol trousers of a cavalry regiment with a yellow stripe down the side and a pair of box spurs sprang into my mind.)

"He wasn't at all happy at school and I'm not surprised. He seems such a gentle person. He wouldn't survive the rough and tumble of a public school very easily." (He should have tried the r. and t. at Kingsdown Comprehensive with me!)

"However long did he stay, Claire? You seem to have got the history of his life."

"Oh, he came when he had finished work and I asked him to stay for supper. He hadn't even got a coat with him when he got here."

I indicated the empty peg on which I had hung my anorak – "But he had when he left!"

Although I affected to be not best pleased by this development, and I did resent the ease with which Byam was able to win them all, this turned out to be a very agreeable development. He fell into the habit of dropping round and Claire fell into the habit of advising him on his multifarious and nefarious problems. I don't think he fell into the habit of taking her advice, but the three cornered relationship became from that moment a happy one.

When I was leaving school, I resisted my father's assumption that I would follow him into the teaching profession. Claire had not been so adroit. She had put her History degree to use after a year's teacher training in a job in a north London Comprehensive. Hating every minute of her days spent encouraging her pupils to empathise with historical characters, she had spent the evenings writing romances. Her novels were full of shy heroines and dashing heroes who in the last chapter rescued the heroine from the arms of the meretricious charmer who the reader had been deceived into thinking was going to be the winner. Her first book was accepted almost without demur and she had written four more, faithfully following this widely selling formula, each indistinguishable from the last, save that the sexy bits grew steamier and steamier.

Byam read them all with great seriousness and lent them to Heather who lent them to Ron's wife. They all became avid fans and my consequence, warmed by Claire's reflected glory, grew.

Chapter Seven

The Flood (Part Two)

As a matter of fact, I was very glad to have the Prince Of Wales. I had been so busy in the Augean stables, working very much from hand to mouth, mending fences, working always against time, placating clients, dabbing at this job and dabbing at that, with crisis never far around the corner. It was with great relief that I took a pace back from the res angusta domi and turned to what I still considered to be a "real" job.

That is to say a job having quantity surveyors, cost forecasts, engineering services consultants, soil tests, schedules of finishes, schedules of fittings, electrical layout drawings and colour schedules. All the paraphernalia, in fact, that makes the modern building process the cumbersome affair that it has become.

After the matey atmosphere of Suffolk, where everybody, it seemed, was on Christian name terms with everybody else, I even derived a certain amount of austere comfort from the anonymity of a strange Planning Authority and an unknown Building Control, to say nothing of a distant and faceless County Highways Department. The weeks wore on. Fairly early in the proceedings, I had had to abandon my hopeful intention of doing every single drawing myself and, on Ron's advice, had called in some outside help in the form of a competent retired building surveyor of Ron's acquaintance who sketched out the joinery details with mechanical and sadly unimaginative efficiency. I was so glad of this relief that I did not complain.

At the end of this time and in consultation with the Brewery we had hammered out a tender list and in this I was much assisted by Simon. He ran a finger down the list of names supplied by his own building division.

"They're all right... They're not too bad... Never heard of them... They're no damned use! I'm not having them again! What a cheek! They really took us to the cleaners on the last job they did for us. Can they imagine we would have forgotten? Constable Construction? I've heard of them (who hasn't?) but are they any good I wonder?" and so on.

We ended up with a list of six contractors. We put all the names in a hat. Ron and his wife, Claire and I, Byam and Heather, all subscribed a pound and each drew a name with the agreement that whoever's nominee put in the lowest price would scoop the pool and we sat down to wait.

In the old days – in the *very* old days that is, even before Sir Hastings' early days, the system was for all the contractors to be invited together with the building owner to a ceremony at which tenders were opened in the Architect's office. This, I suppose, to ensure that there was no chicanery. One can well imagine the scene. It must have been desperately embarrassing and I was thankful that these days were long in the past. On this occasion we had arranged for the tenders to be delivered to the Brewery and the quantity surveyor and I, Simon, the Brewery Surveyor and the Chairman of the Company duly foregathered at twelve noon on the due day.

This is a bad moment for quantity surveyors. With perpetually rising building costs, their task of providing an accurate cost forecast is an unenviable one. Still less enviable is the experience of standing by registering icy calm while the envelopes are opened, putting them wrong by ten, by fifteen, by twenty percent and improvising in their minds an explanation for why this should be so.

The meeting was held in the Chairman's office. Five glasses and a bottle of Pouilly Fuissé were standing on the table with a pile of pink envelopes beside them. The Chairman who, on his Olympian height, was not professionally or even emotionally involved in the outcome, proceeded to open the envelopes -

"Barraclough and Sons .... £624,523"

The quantity surveyor, whose preliminary forecast had been a little under £500,000 assumed a rictus smile.

"Mowbray and Gladstone," continued the Chairman, "£607,400.

"Braddock Construction... £506,000.

"R. Woodruffe Ltd... £516,042.

"Constable Construction... £493,420.

"Mangreve Masters (1985)... £586,425.

"My wife"ll be pleased," I said.

"Why so?"

"She drew Constable in the office sweep."

"Well," said the Chairman, "it looks like Constable Construction then?" Then he added vaguely, "Price all right, is it? Is that what we were expecting?"

"Not too bad," said the Quantity Surveyor in a neutral voice, though I could see that he was relieved, if not to say quietly triumphant, at the result. "Anything under £500,000... We would, of course, have preferred to be in the middle somewhere, but that's not too bad.

"What do we know about Constable Construction?" asked the Chairman.

"They're all right," said Simon hurriedly, because he had, indeed, recommended their inclusion himself. "We've used them before. No problems as far as I remember."

"Constable are stable, Constable are able.
Constable Construction for all your building needs." I said, quoting the boring advertising jingle of this much publicised company.

"I remember them of old," said the Chairman, "when old John Constable was alive and his son – Tom was it? – was killed in a car smash. Tragic. The old man lost heart after that and I don't know anything about them since they were taken over."

"Very efficient. Lots of hype," said the Brewery Surveyor disparagingly. I could see he didn't like the firm very much and wondered why. He continued, "I'm sorry it wasn't Braddocks though, but there you are."

We settled down to congratulate each other, to toast the success of the contract, to reaffirm arrangements made for the temporary housing of Derek Laker and to head the Chairman off from a last minute suggestion that it would be perfectly possible to keep the Prince Of Wales open while works were in hand. Towards the end of this I found myself beside the Brewery Surveyor, "You don't like Constable much, do you?" I said.

"No, not much. Though, I don't know, perhaps I'm being unfair. They've only done one job for us since they reorganised themselves, but they tried to pull a fast one, or so I thought. It wasn't the easiest job in the world and we didn't have a very good set of drawings. Specification wasn't up to much either, so perhaps it wasn't entirely their fault, but I certainly got the impression that nobody could teach Constable Construction much when it comes to a contractual claim."

I was to remember his words.

In due course, the Quantity Surveyor's cost check on Constable's priced bill of quantities came back to us, revealing mathematical errors of no more than a few pounds, and, in due course, we entered into a contract with that firm. I had spent the intervening period neurotically studying the bill of quantities and my drawings, painfully aware of the warning I had received as to the business methods of Constable and wondering, of course, what I had forgotten.

I spent a good deal of time printing drawings, duplicate copies of every drawing we had prepared for a very large number of people. I even briefly sighed nostalgically for the London Borough of Bow where some junior would have been available to stand in a haze of ammonia beside the die-line printer, unattractively underlit by its blue light. No junior at Spring House, only myself. My consolation, though, throughout as the printed procession of drawings emerged, was that, the more I looked at it, the more I thought my scheme was a good one.

And so the job started on site. Fortnightly site meetings became the story of my life, with occasional unscheduled site visits in between and the journey to Stevendon became wearisomely familiar. The personalities on site became wearisomely familiar too.

I soon realised the truth of the Brewery Surveyor's comment about Constable's expertise in handling a contractual claim. No set of drawings is perfect and no firm of contractors faultless. Unscrupulous contractors can, and do, search out the weaknesses in the contract documents and exploit them, to the discomfiture of the Architect and, by these means, discreetly pave the way for claims for extensions of contract time and increases in cost. If they feel they are slipping behind schedule, they will call for a mass of unnecessary additional detail and, if the issue of this be delayed, duly register the fact.

In these circumstances, the Architect's footwork needs to be nimble indeed and I became disturbingly aware, as time went by, that in the early days of the contract, I had, through overwork, or laziness, or good nature even, let several of these occasions pass unchecked and become a matter of record.

The site agent at the Prince Of Wales was a certain Norman Hawkins, a man who, in the opinion of Claire, to whom I had described his physical appearance, sported a large walrus moustache in order to conceal an inadequate personality. He was hand in glove with the foreman carpenter who – since the job was carpentry intensive, was an unusually important figure. These two together became (of course) the Walrus and the Carpenter in my mind and I detested them both impartially.

I wished I had Ron's easy and insouciant confidence in handling the time-consuming enquiries which were the Walrus's method of wrongfooting the Architect. Just occasionally, if I was out, he would pick up the telephone and speak to the Walrus direct and on one or two occasions I overheard a refreshing exchange similar to the following -

"Steel'ere. Naw, Mr. Simpson's out. You'll have to deal with me. You want what? What's yer bill reference?" Then, "35 L to Q inclusive is it? Let's 'ave a look. Hum, hum, hum. Yer, rafter sizes, yer, ceiling joist sizes, yer. Eaves height shown on the drawings is it? Yer... " And then, explosively, "For God's sake! It's all there, isn't it? You don't want a detail for that! My Aunt Fanny could build the bloody thing in an afternoon with 'er Meccano set on the information here for Christ's sake!" Pause and then -

"Three points for you then – one, I'm *not* going to refer it to Mr. Simpson. Two, no we're *not* going to issue a detail. Three, no I'm *not* going to give you an order. Four, just get on with it and don't waste our time! Got it?"

The Walrus, whose patronising and derisive attitudes were as a rule able to reduce me to subservient compliance with his every whim, had never been spoken to in that vein before and Ron, becoming aware of me standing at the door behind him, turned to me and said seriously,

"You want to watch these Constable characters, Jack. That Walrus of yours is as cute as a rat! I've had these barrack room lawyers before. I know the type. Hold out a finger and they'll take your arm off at the shoulder. Bloody sharks! Let them do some of the jumping."

It was easy for Ron; as Byam and I often said to each other – he knew it all, but, under his breezy guidance, the job progressed, I became more confident. I outsmarted some of Constables' more obvious manoeuvres, but I was uneasily aware that in the early days of the contract I had left some time bombs ticking away for my ultimate discomfiture. When the contract started I had, well almost, given up smoking, but as it drew into its forty second week or thereabouts I was back, to Claire's distress, on twenty a day.

After a three hour work out with the Walrus and the Carpenter in vociferous form and the back-up squad from Constables' head office in the person of Mr. Smyles (so inaptly named), their quantity surveyor, I needed tranquility and a Gauloise. I would sit uneasily at these site meetings, my site note pad beside me, numbering off the things I ought to do the minute I got back, uncomfortably aware that Claire and I were going out to dinner that night and trying desperately to remember when I had actually issued the final instruction in respect of carpeting in the bedrooms (if it was on the 'first schedule' well and good, if on the second – yet another claim for time extension).

The job was, though, by no means without its compensations. Simon became an indispensable ally and some of his caustic interventions at the site meetings which he occasionally attended were very useful to me indeed. He knew exactly when to make some discreet reference to further works pending for the Brewery and managed, without saying so, to suggest that, if all went well on the Prince of Wales, the far more extensive remodelling of the Brewery might well be the subject of a negotiated contract with Constables. He let it be inferred that the entire board of Melfords were watching the progress of events and in particular the final account on the Prince of Wales, with unabated interest.

Another consolation, and that of a more solid sort, derived from the development of the building itself. The brick I had selected so many months before was even better than it had seemed when I had inspected it in the stack. The colour of the pointing, the subject of furious debate with the Walrus, was well worth the trouble I had taken to get it exactly right. The thin balusters on the eliptical balcony over the entrance, and which I had feared were at too narrow an interval, were just right, the very slight batter, which at much trouble I had imparted to the principal chimney stack was worth every one of the many pennies which it had cost. The little house, now shorn of its later alterations, was obviously going to be a worthy object in itself.

Claire and I went down one sunny Sunday and sat on the wall of what would be the terrace and, like God in Genesis Chapter 1, saw that it was good. While we sat congratulating ourselves, to my great surprise, a familiar Mercedes swished into the yard and Simon stepped out, accompanied by an elderly figure, no less elegant than himself. They stood in green wellingtons, waxed jackets and flat caps like a couple of gentleman farmers at a point to point, before good manners came to his rescue. He seemed embarrassed to see me.

"Jack, what on earth are you doing here? Don't you ever take the weekend off? Let me introduce ... this is Brigadier Molyneux. Sir, let me introduce Jack Simpson, our architect."

"This is my wife. Claire, may I introduce Simon Melford."

We shook hands and said things like "Well, well, well," and "How do you think it's looking?" And, to the Brigadier, "Did you see it before?"

The Brigadier said things like, "No," and "Yes," and "Jolly good!"

After a while, Simon said, "Look here, Jack, this is terribly confidential, but the Brigadier is an equerry to..." He mentioned a very exalted personage. "And there is a chance,"

"Better than a chance," interjected the Brigadier.

"All right then, better than a chance, that the Prince might come down and open the pub. He's concerned with the new town; this is his sort of thing and he's got to be in Steventon on the 24th of July. That's a fortnight after the contract completion date, but, before we get too far with this, it has to be finished. Finished, like 'finished' Jack, if you understand me. It would be a tremendous thing for the Prince of Wales, for the town, for the district, for me, for you and even for Constables I dare say! Can it be done? We've got another six weeks. I should have thought that ought to be all right. Bar counter looks nice, by the way. What do you say?"

At this moment Derek Laker, emerging from his half completed flat into which we had moved him about a fortnight before, came briskly across the site. "What about it Jack? Don't see any problem myself. Can't be a problem anyway – the wife's bought a new hat." Hearty laughter. Everyone looked at me.

"Six weeks Simon," I said, "A fortnight over contract time. They've got extensions of time beyond that, you know. I don't know. I'll have to think. When do you have to know?"

"By the end of the week," said the Brigadier.

I didn't think I was making a very good showing.

Claire came and stood close behind me and pinched my hand between finger and thumb encouragingly and with more confidence than I felt I said, "I'm sure we can do it. No – no problem. Leave it to me. I'll just check a thing or two with Constables and ring you in the morning. Pencil it in for now, but I'm sure we can ink it in tomorrow."

"How's your boil?" asked Claire.

"I think it's getting bigger. Yes...", after a glance in the driving mirror, "yes, it's getting bigger."

On the following day and at what at first Constables were prepared derisively to consider to be impossibly short notice, I summoned a meeting of those principally concerned at six o'clock in the Brewery offices. There were, on their side, the Walrus, their quantity surveyor, a Constable Director, the contract manager and on my side myself and Simon.

We listed the work yet to be done. We spoke of delays on special finishes. We agreed that the decoration of the bottle store could be omitted. We agreed that the garages could not be finished in time, but they were so discreetly sited that this wouldn't matter. We worried about deliveries on the pavings and we asked each other questions about the commissioning of the heating. The Walrus, true to form, had come with his customary list of late information required from the architect but was peremptorily waved into silence by the Constable Director who even said, with a steely glitter in his eye, and impatiently, "I'm sure you can get round that. And anyway, we're relying on you."

Hardly was this meeting over when announcements began to appear in the press. Television cameras arrived and viewed our so nearly completed building. Advocates of what is so inaccurately known as 'temperance' expressed their disapproval. Flags and bunting were ordered. I stopped eating or sleeping. My boil got bigger. Another one appeared.

Five weeks after the momentous encounter with the Brigadier, it really seemed that we had made it. We locked the office one day and Claire and I went down once more with Heather and Byam and Ron. Without doubt, they were impressed.

"Bloody marvellous, old boy!" said Byam.

"Turned out all right, hasn't it?" said Ron.

"Very nice," said Heather.

Derek set out five pints in a row and one for himself and proposed a toast of confusion to Constable and success to the Prince of Wales.

Pride, however went before a fall. The following morning I had perhaps the most devastating telephone call in my life.

It was, of course, the voice of the Walrus. Not his familiar derisive tone, but something verging on hysteria.

"We've got water coming up through the floor of the cellar.

Commissioned the boiler yesterday. Came in this morning and found it standing in a foot of water. We're pumping but it's coming in as fast as we can pump it out." And then, ominously, "You'd better get down here!"

Pausing only to leave a note to Ron to say where I was and what had happened, I cut ten minutes off my record time to Stevendon and found the grim assembly on site. The cellar was dry but in the sump a submersible pump with a hose led out through the cellar flaps to the pond.

"Knock the pump off!" shouted the Walrus and, as the clatter died away, with hideous stealth, the water began to bubble up through the floor and within a very few minutes we were standing in an inch of water, the sump was full and the level was still rising.

"Something's gone wrong with the tanking," I said desperately.

"Nothing wrong with the tanking," said a shadowy figure, who, up till that moment I had not identified, and who turned out to be a representative of the asphalt company responsible for this part of the work. "Nothing wrong with the tanking, I can tell you!

"But where's it coming from?" I asked, nonplussed. "The excavation was perfectly dry."

"It wasn't, you know," said the Walrus with grim triumph. "Do you remember, when we did the digging we came across a seam of ballast? Over there in the corner it was," he pointed. "Drew your attention to it at the time. All this rain we've had – that little ballast fault must be running like a stream. I warned you."

"Is that true, Mr. Simpson?" asked the contracts manager. "If so, the implications are serious. Very serious indeed. Our company can't be held responsible. You'll have to notify the Brewery, to say nothing of the Palace. We won't be held responsible for this, you know."

"I didn't think the inner leaf was strong enough on the east side. That should have been 225 at least," said an anonymous voice from the back of the meeting.

I shook myself. I collected what remained of my thoughts.

"Get a Kango down here," I said. "Get some brickwork cut out over there. Let's have a look at the tanking."

"There's hydrostatic pressure out there ... "

"The walls weren't designed to take that."

"I did warn you ..."

"Reinforced concrete inner wall... waterproof rendering..." "Floor surface not thick enough ... is there any reinforcement in it?"

And the recurring theme, "Can't get anything done in the time."

The crowd in the cellar was now augmented by the arrival of a bricklayer and labourer who proceeded to attack the wall, extracting four bricks which fell with a squashy splash into the rising water.

"Turn that bloody pump on again!" shouted the Walrus and the clamour of suggestion and counter suggestion and accusation was drowned out by the urgent clamour of that beastly little pump.

I peered through the hole in the brickwork through which like the ebony buttock of a Hottentot Venus, the asphalt bulged in a disconcerting way. I pressed my ear to it and from within came a watery sound like a kiss, a prehistoric kiss, a kiss from the Pleistocene age. I began to form a grim opinion as to what had, in fact, gone wrong.

"Get a hole drilled in that," I said with more incision than I felt and the Carpenter appeared, in his hand a gleaming brace and bit.

"Hole there, please," I said in my authoratitive voice, pointing to the middle of the hole.

The Carpenter applied the point of his bit and began to turn. Flakes of asphalt scattered into the water and then, with a dramatic suddenness, a jet of pure spring water leapt from the wall a distance of about five feet, hitting the Carpenter full in the stomach and filling the pocket of his apron. Up till then it had not been a satisfactory morning but this was at least a satisfactory moment.

"Shit!" said the Carpenter, leaping back, wiping his eyes and emptying his pocket.

"Only thing you can do," said the asphalt man, "is let the cellar fill up, with the pressure you've got out there. You're going to lose the wall if you don't!"

The hair on the back of my neck crawled. "I think," I thought, "I'll just pop upstairs, get into the car and drive home to Lavenham and when I get there I'll have a cup of tea and spend the rest of the day in bed with Claire."

At this impasse, Derek Laker appeared on the stairs, "Telephone, Jack."

"I can't come now Derek," I said.

"It's Mr. Steel. He said I was to fetch you. He said it was urgent."

On reflection I thought at least it would get me away for a while and I stumbled my way up the stairs. The meeting trailed damply after me and gathered like so many Marabout storks nodding sagely on the terrace.

I picked up the so recently installed wall telephone behind the bar. "Jack?" said Ron's voice. "Got a bit of bother have you? I've been talking to the landlord, so I think I know all about it. Looks like you need a bit of dewatering. I've been through the file. I think I know what the problem is... In fact, I'm sure I do. That little seam of ballast? Constable wrote to you about it, oh, back in November sometime. Got the letter 'ere. But that's not the point and anyway... I've put my thinking cap on and I reckon this – that seam of ballast, it must have come from somewhere and what's more, it must go somewhere. I've spoken to the geological survey blokes in Cambridge. You've only got to go about a mile down Shephall Hill and chalk is practically outcrop. Looks like you've only got about thirty feet of clay overburden. Then what? Chalk, me old son! That's where your little ballast number's off to! Into the chalk. It isn't a problem really. All you've got to do is pull the plug out! Sink a bore hole down into the chalk; site'll be bone dry before you can say action for negligence."

"Ron, you may be right and you may be wrong, but – Christ! – we've got exactly a week before the opening and," I added pathetically, lowering my voice, "you've no conception what a mad-house it is here today."

"Yer, and it's been a bit of a mad-house back at the home farm too, I can tell you! Bloody telephone! That's really why I haven't been able to get in touch before and – look – I know you've only got a week and that's why I've done a bit of arranging. There's a bloke called Thundridge, Jimmy Thundridge, known him for years. Done a lot of work for us – two or three places where there wasn't a decent water supply and we had to drop a bore – no, he's all right, Jimmy. I rang him and, as luck would have it, this blessed day, if you can believe, at this blessed moment even, he's moving a rig from a site about two miles from you. Glad enough not to have to take it back to the yard! What's the time now? Yer, he'll be with you in about half an hour, I'd guess, so you'd better get out there!

"Ron, for Christ's sake, what are you saying? That a drilling rig will be here in about half an hour and all set to drop a bore? Will it work?"

"Oh, yer, it'll work all right and – I say, Jack, I've just been looking at your plan, drawing number thirtysomething. Remember it? You've got a note there – 'Existing brick walling retained'. Remember it? Well – get four paving stones taken up on the word 'brick' – that looks about the best place to me. Easy access and, if I read it right, just on top of your little ballast number and – Jack – is there a digger on site?"

I looked out of the window. "Yes, there's a Drot. Why?"

"And a dumper truck? Two? Better still! Why? Well what goes down has to come up if you take my meaning! As soon as Jimmy starts drilling, you're going to have enough mud on your fancy terrace to rebuild the Great Wall of China! You might as well move it as it accumulates otherwise a certain exalted personnage will wish he'd worn his wellies after all when he comes next week."

"Ron, you're a genius! Thank God ...."

"Gawn! Tell you what, Jack, I wouldn't mind seeing the fun! And in the meantime, don't let these Constable characters put anything over on you. And while you're waiting I should have a scotch. 'Clean, bright and slightly oiled", that's the specification on these occasions. See ya!" And he was gone.

"Won the pools have you?" said Derek Laker who had been standing beside me and watching carefully.

"God, Derek," I said frankly, "I really don't know, but we're very soon going to find out."

Derek eyed me speculatively, "Little drink wouldn't do you any harm, I think. Wouldn't do me any harm, either."

Three drinks, seven Gauloises and forty minutes later, during which time I had persuaded the reluctant Walruss to dismantle the pavings suggested by Ron and to assemble the Drot and its attendant dumpers, Jimmy Thundridge, as bright and bird-like as Ron himself, had arrived with his rig on a low loader. I had silenced the protests of Constable who were deeply indignant at the arrival, under no sort of contract with themselves, of an independent operator, and who were muttering ominously about the insurance position and eloquent as to their total dissociation from the consequences of what I proposed, and baffled at the speed with which my arrangements had been made which as far as they were concerned were the fruit of one five minute telephone conversation.

Jimmy Thundridge, on the other hand, saw no problem of any sort at all. He nodded sagely as I outlined Ron's diagnosis and referred reassuringly to similar problems in the immediate locality. He brushed aside my sotto voce question about the possible cost ("Hundreds rather than thousands") and lost no time at all in erecting the rig over the dismantled pavings.

The entire company of Marabout storks stood in silence on the newly completed terrace walling, their shoulders hunched against the persistent rain which had begun to fall. I took my station beside Jimmy Thundridge and he briskly began the drilling with a rapped out, "OK, Pete, start her up!"

The drill began to turn and mud, as Ron had predicted, began to spew in astonishing quantities across the terrace. A hand fell on my shoulder.

"Hope it works, Jack."

"Without turning round I held up two crossed fingers. "So do I, Simon!" I said.

The drill turned on, the mud accumulated, the Drot scooped it up and the dumpers scampered away to tip it at the end of the site. The whole scene took on the appearance of a sand pit game. A line of Lego men on the terrace wall, Lego machinery bustling away in the sand pit. Jimmy Thundridge turned to me and said something which above the clatter I could not hear. From his expression it seemed to be good news. I nodded and smiled first to him and then, with a reassurance I did not feel, to Simon.

At first, the clay which came up with about the consistency of porridge was a grey-blue, unattractively flecked with yellow. After what seemed a very long time indeed but which Derek was later to tell me was only about a quarter of an hour, there was a slight change in the rubbish mounding round our feet. Little flecks of white began to appear. I made the mistake of picking one up and was immersed to the elbow in mud before I could snatch my hand away. The white flecks became more frequent, much more frequent. Soon large chunks of what looked for all the world like the best blackboard chalk was churned out round our feet. Jimmy put his mouth close to my ear, "Ten metres," he shouted. "Mr. Steel wasn't far wrong."

I slipped away to the open cellar flaps and climbed down the rolling way into the cellar where an inspection lamp fixed to a heating pipe illuminated a depressing scene. I reached down and, with the fleck of chalk between finger and thumb, marked the water level on the wall and, as I did so, Simon joined me.

"Who's fault, Jack?" he said.

"I don't know," I said miserably, "Mine perhaps. But look, Simon, look at that!"

Almost unbelievably, the water began to shiver and, before our eyes, to fall. Soon my chalk mark was one brick course above the water level and then two and then, amazingly, a floor slab appeared. "Well, bugger me!" he said.

I sank onto the bottom step of the cellar stair. I had an awful suspicion I was going to be sick. Simon, however, burst into roars of laughter. "I'm never going to forget this! What a scene! Well done you! What a bloody miracle! When Constable rang this morning, you'd have thought it was the end of the world – now it just looks like day one after the Flood."

My weakness left me and was replaced by a deep and all-embracing satisfaction.

When we rejoined the party on the terrace, Jimmy Thundridge had already knocked off the rig and I was able to confront the reproachful glare of the Walrus with boundless satisfaction.

"All right, Noah," I said crisply to him, "You can fly off a dove now if you want to. And you might as well get this lot washed down and when the rig's gone, you can get the pavings put down again.

"Going down, is it?" asked Jimmy.

"Gone!" I said.

"Where do you want us to send our account?"

As I was preparing to answer, a familiar red Cavalier drew up in the yard. Ron stepped out, fastidiously changing his shoes for Derry boots and covering his red head with a trilby hat, advanced across the site shrugging his way into his macintosh as he came.

"Where do you want the account sent, Mr. Steel?" asked Jimmy again.

"Constable, of course," said Ron. "Where else?" And turning to the walrus, "Drawing shows the asphalt on the *face* of the wall, right? Found it bulged when you cut a bit away did you? Know why? Because it wasn't properly grouted when you built the inner wall. Nothing wrong with the tanking, either, as far as I know, but when it's on the face of the wall like that, leave a gap and it's likely to break up with any sort of hydrostatic pressure! Yers, send your bill to Constable, Jimmy!"

Chapter Eight

The Wedding.

Most of my friends and contemporaries were working in London and elsewhere in large architectural practices and on important contracts. They had all more or less become one job men and their jobs lasted for two, three, four or even more years. Their clients were Local Authorities or corporations, public or semi-public bodies and, as such, were pretty faceless. Not so at Spring House! And, although I occasionally sighed for the ordered beat and the dignified development of a contract where costs are measured in millions, it has to be admitted that there were advantages in the variety of the things we had to deal with. We became – and in this as in all things guided by Ron – shrewd judges of the probable form of new clients.

"'Ello, 'ello," Ron would say. "Not sure if I like the look of that. Looks as if we've got another Mrs. Cartwright on our hands!"

Or Byam would say, "Not much of a job, but I think I'll jog it along – it could be another Ponsonby."

Semi-seriously, notable clients were remembered in a series of annual awards. Heather took these *very* seriously and would get quite annoyed if her nominees were ever jostled into second or third place. Thus we established the prestigious Tallent Cup for the 'Shit of the Year', remembering by this the evil machinations of a notably crooked property developer. The Lady Sherwood Memorial Vase for 'The Most Spoilt Lady of the Year' recalled from the distant past an incident still green in the memories of Ron and Heather. There was the John Carter medal for 'The Best Vicar of the Year', the Bell & Son Cup for 'The Best Builder of the Year' and, finally, the Lindsay Ross Plate for 'The Outstanding Client of the Year'.

By these devices we kept our sanity, though we feared that one day a winner would come in and see the neatly typed list on the wall in Heather's office.

As time went by, Byam and I began to feel that we had begun to understand the inbuilt characteristics that made for a good, or for a bad, client and worked out the following list -

Good.	*Bad.*
Bank Managers	Accountants
Estate Agents	Land Agents
The Retired Military	Retired Air Force
Nuns	Dons
The impoverished nobility and gentry	The prosperous nobility and gentry

Those born under the sign of Scorpio and Leo

Those born under the sign of Gemini and Pisces

When Lt. Col. (Retd.) Lindsay Ross appeared in our lives we thought he sounded promising. When a quick look in Sir Hastings' 'Who's Who' told us he was born on the 3rd of August our early expectations seemed sound and when he revealed himself as being without doubt of the gentry and impoverished with it, we felt that it was confirmed. We were right; he was to give his name to our award for the Best Client of the Year.

At his invitation, and using the opportunity of being out together and in that part of the county anyway, Byam and I went together to call. The Colonel's house – Oak Farm, Little Hampden in the north of the county, looked like nothing so much as a tea cosy – a thatched tea cosy. In its Medieval origins, it was a 'hall house', that is to say that it had once had a central hall extending up into the roof with a two storey cross wing at either end. The hall was now floored over but Medieval evidences were widespread; there were diamond mullioned windows, the grooves for shutters (though these had disappeared) and a fine pair of screens arches. Whether by instinct or lack of funds, the Colonel had not disturbed the original brick floor and the centre of the house was occupied by enormous back to back fire-places. The Colonel had evidently lost a number of old fruit trees in the previous year's gales. There was a huge stock of fruit wood logs by the back door and one, distilling its smokey incense through the house, smouldered on the hearth.

"Don't call me Sir," he said reprovingly to Byam, "Not in the army now. Call me Tom. Good of you fellows to come. Take a seat and smoke if you want to."

It must have been some years since he had last issued battalion orders and he was in his element. His dining room table was, as it were, laid for four with a neat set of typed notes in front of each place and a coffee pot with its attendant cups and saucers dressed by the right.

"Now then – Information. The house is in my wife's name so the contracting party will be Iris Lindsay Ross. I've got £20,000 to spend and that must be inclusive of architect's fee and VAT and all the rub-bish. Just had a legacy from my brother. Sooner have him than the legacy, of course, but it was very decent of him. Didn't have to leave me anything... My daughter – that's my youngest daughter – is get-ting married next September so we must be finished by then. Got plenty of time but I don't suppose I need to tell you that it soon slips away. Do help yourselves to coffee."

Iris sat by with a pad in front of her and it wouldn't be fair to say that she had an indulgent smile but it could be said that it was only with care that she did not have an indulgent smile.

"Intention. One. To renew the roof covering on the barn. At the moment it's covered in corrugated iron – colander iron I call it, it's so full of holes – and you chaps will have to advise me as to the best material, bearing in mind the cash limit. Two. We need a second bathroom. We've only got one at the moment. Grubby little place."

"Oh, come on, Tom! It's not as bad as all that!" said Iris.

"Well, show you in a minute. You be the judge. Getting a bit old for a ground floor bathroom so we thought we'd build out a new one over the kitchen lean-to, what they call the "outshot". Three, and we shall only do this if the cash holds out, so you can consider it of secondary priority – we get a bit of trouble from time to time with the drains. It doesn't happen all the time, only when there's a lot of people staying in the house and it's been raining, but – you get a couple of baths on the run and it's apt to back up. The third bath and there's water on the kitchen floor. Shouldn't be a problem but people don't always take trouble." His mild blue eye roamed over his wife for a moment and he continued,

"Method. Well, of course, that's where you fellows come in..."

We talked about a measured survey, we talked about architect's fees, we made an aproximation of the cost (it didn't look as if it was going to be too bad). As time – when we came to work it out – did not seem to be entirely on our side, we agreed in the first instance to negotiate a price with a local contractor. Luckily one of the best was based only ten miles away. Horses for courses, naturally, and we could just imagine this particular contractor, who was relaxed, informal and efficient, getting on very well with the Colonel.

We set out on a tour of the estate. The house was shabby and the furniture old and comfortable and nothing much matched anything else. The curtains had been both shortened and lengthened and seemed to write the history of the Colonel's military career as he moved from one quarter to the next. The pictures wrote his career too. There were Snaffles drawings of Indian soldiers, Lionel Edwards prints of point to points, framed photographs in which Tom and sometimes Iris grew steadily older and here and there little bits of silver added little bits of post script -

"On the occasion of his marriage" ... "On transfer" ... "On promotion" ... and, of course, finally, "On retirement".

The house may have been shabby but the garden was meticulous. Everything that could be labelled was labelled; everything in the toolshed was in its proper place and everything seemed to have been polished. Vegetables stood on parade, their thumbs, it seemed, in line with the seams of their trousers. The barn, the reroofing of which formed part one of paragraph two above, as the Colonel put it, was a fine, stout-hearted little seventeenth century structure, its weatherboard kept carefully in repair and its roof timbers seemingly sound enough despite the speckle of sunshine through the many holes in the corrugated iron.

The job remained what the Colonel called 'a combined op.'. I did the survey, Byam did the preliminary drawings; I did the working drawings, Ron wrote the specification and Tom read and studied everything with close attention. The contractor's estimate wasn't far wide of our preliminary forecast and, as we had guessed, he and Tom got on like a house on fire. Sadly, a considerable death watch beetle infestation in the roof timbers pushed the price up to a point where phase three, paragraph two – that is to say the work to the drains was, perforce, postponed. An ominous decision, had we known!

The job went admirably from the start. As we had hoped, the Colonel and the contractor became good friends; Tom visited the site two or three times a day, full of gratitude and admiration, Iris popped across with a tray laden with buns, biscuits and coffee at least twice a day and the about-to-be-married daughter paid the boys on site a good deal of flattering attention.

Byam and I, having discovered that you could get a cup of coffee any time between ten and twelve, lunch any time between twelve and two and a large drink any time between five and seven, paid the job a good deal of flattering attention too. The Colonel had an attractive way of putting vegetables or fruit or even a dozen eggs or a bottle of home-made wine in the boot for us – "Seem to have got more eggs than we can get through this week... Wondered if you'd like to try the elderflower (bit soon to be drinking it but I think it's going to be good)... Really ought to eat these little turnips before they get woody, don't you know." And so on. We sent him an account from time to time and were embarrassed by the speed with which these were settled. Never by post – always by hand. He would arrive at Spring House and with a quick "haven't come to disturb you fellows" would make his way to call on Heather whose unstinted approval he had gained very early on in the proceedings by addressing her as Miss Mills.

"Good morning, Miss Mills. Happened to be in Lavenham. Thought I'd get this settled. Well, thank you... if you're making one... just one sugar. Brought you a few roses. Brighten the place up?" And after a precise ten minute he went on his way. "Got to get the chickens moved."

In due course, the bathroom was completed (the little gabled extension over the kitchen outshot) and the barn was reroofed. We were well satisfied with our efforts. In good time the barn was swept out and ready for the wedding reception and its following dance.

"Can't think why they need to have a dance," said the Colonel in puzzlement. "Would never have thought of such a thing when I was young, but it seems to be all the go now."

And in due course the invitations arrived. Colonel and Mrs. Lindsay Ross requested the pleasure of the company of Mr. and Mrs. Simpson and of Mr. Alexander and friend at the wedding of their daughter...

At this point I have to digress to explain "and friend". I had for some time been aware of a certain nuance in Byam's life. Disappearances to distant weekends, an upgrading of the already considerable wardrobe, an alternation between care and elation, the sudden disappearance of his moustache ("Such a shame! Can't imagine what he can have been thinking of!" said Heather.) And Byam, usually tediously forthcoming in respect of his sentimental life, became uncharacteristically reticent. All was, however, one day revealed.

"You'll never guess what I saw outside the office today!" I said to Claire.

"Don't tell me!... Let me guess... the Salvation Army band playing for Sir Hastings' birthday?"

"No – a red Ferrari! And you'll never guess who was inside it!"

"Madonna?... Gazza?... Luciano Pavarotti?... The Chairman and Secretary of the District Council Resources Committee in horrible embrace?"

"Well, the windows were so steamed up, it was at first quite hard to see but, I'm sure I saw, in the passenger seat, Mr. Alexander and, in the driver's seat, none other than... Gentian Woodruffe! Ho, ho!"

"Who on earth's Gentian Woodruffe?"

"Can you have forgotten? She's the girl in the flashy car I saw on the first day I came to call on Sir H. The one I sent off to Pam's Pantry. He hasn't mentioned her since so I rather thought I'd ruined their romance."

That same evening, as it happened, Byam chose to call at the Pottergate on his way home and, finding Claire alone, became at once the subject of an in-depth enquiry which was still in progress when I got home. They were both sitting perched in the kitchen, Byam moodily stirring a cup of coffee and Claire ironing and interrogating. There was a good deal of 'So then what did you do?.. Oh, did you?.. Good move I should think... And what did she say?.. Mm, don't like the sound of that much!.. Why don't you..? It sounds to me as though you're being a bit too abject..." And so on. I was clearly not wanted at this summit but I heard all about it later.

"Well, I must say, she sounds quite nice. Byam's obviously very smitten. They had a bit of a swing round year ago, then she went off to San Francisco for the winter and there was this other chap. Didn't like the sound of him much. But then she rang Byam up and they went to a May Ball together. I think he was something of a stop gap but, obviously, he made good use of his time – she gave him a first edition of 'When We Were Very Young' for Christmas, you know – 'Wherever I am, there's always Pooh' and all that. I thought that was very significant, don't you? Anyway, we'll see because she's coming to the wedding hand in hand with the dashing Alexander.

"I really think he's quite serious but she's frightfully rich – he'd like that, of course, but it does set a problem because I gather that Daddy Woodruffe is very disapproving. When Byam went to stay there, silly ass, he ran out of money and had to borrow a fiver. Not the most propitious start in the world and, anyway, I understand Mr. Woodruffe doesn't approve of architects. Byam says lots of big contractors don't."

"Big contractors? Good Lord! Is he Woodruffe Construction? Then there really is a bit of money about! Trust old Byam!"

In the second week of September we made our way to Little Hampden for the Ross wedding. It had been raining, raining to a point where Byam and I, mindful of the effect of the new bathroom and a houseful of people on the Colonel's dubious sewage disposal arrangements, had begun to worry. The day was brilliantly fine and warm, the church was stuffed to the roof with the last of the Colonel's summer flowers and packed to the doors with the Colonel's friends and relations.

Claire shed several tears and so did the Colonel and the bride looked enchanting. Gentian, though, it must be admitted, momentarily stole the show. Making the latest possible entrance before the bride, she drifted down the aisle on Byam's arm in a haze of cowslip yellow silk, smiling reassuringly to left and right at the questioning eyebrows and favouring familiar faces in the crowd with an intensification of the glow from her cornflower blue eyes. I felt both irritated and honoured when she dropped a light kiss on my right cheek and sank silkily into the pew next to me. Claire grunted something unfathomable, the organ struck up and the wedding began.

When we returned that evening for the dance she was wearing, rather suitably I thought, a full and colourfully embroidered skirt and peasant blouse and Byam his deceptively simple white Armani suit. We met them in the lane and strolled down through the lines of parked cars to the barn which was glowing with candlelight and beginning to thump with music. The house was like an overturned ants' nest and, as far as I could count, about a dozen large Suffolk ladies were toiling in the kitchen and as many Suffolk maidens were running backwards and forwards between the house and the barn with trays. A small van had just delivered an enormous block of ice and the Colonel emerged from the front door with this clasped in his arms, insecurely wrapped in about twenty copies of the Eastern Daily Press. Two of his sons-in-law followed him through the front door, armed improbably with mops and buckets.

"Drains are giving us a bit of a problem," he said without preamble. "All those baths, all this rain, ditches full. Backing up as fast as we can mop it. Still, all the girls are doing wonders."

We peered through the door and, indeed, the kitchen was awash. There must have been, despite the efforts of the sons-in-law mopping amongst the legs of the toiling Suffolk ladies, four inches of water over the whole of the kitchen floor.

"Is there a plumber in the house?" asked Gentian in her rather maddening little voice.

"No, no plumber, I'm afraid," said the Colonel.

"But there are two architects," said Claire. "Can't you do something?", rounding on us.

"Well, er..." said Byam dubiously, eyeing his white suit. "Not much you can do really..."

"At least you could have a look," said Claire.

"You could poke a stick down it or something," encouraged Gentian, "Come on! Call yourselves architects?"

"Well at least we could have a look," I said with an attempt at brightness. "With a hundred people on the premises, and all drinking," – another tray laden with brimming beer glasses swished by us – "somebody had better do something quickly."

"Nothing whatever you can do, of course," said the Colonel, "but, well, if you could just have a *look* to see if you can identify the problem, well, I'd be most grateful. You'll have to excuse me now ..."

The hospitable noises from the barn grew in tempo and he turned to Claire and Gentian, "Come along me dears. Not your affair. Girls are coping. We'll leave these chaps to it."

Byam and I made our way to the twinned manhole covers of the septic tank just visible in the gloaming under the boughs of a laden apple tree. Distastefully, Byam turned up the bottom of his trousers and meticulously hung his jacket on a nearby branch. I did the same. With a squashy sucking noise, we lifted each manhole cover in turn. From the distant barn came a surge of laughter and the tinkle of a piano, as, followed by a saxophone, it went into 'The Yellow Rose of Texas', while an accordion surged and panted in pursuit.

"'The wedding guest, he beat his breast,
 He heard the loud bassoon,'" said Byam. "And while we're on the subject, you could add,
'And slimy things did crawl with legs
Upon a slimy sea.'"

It was all too true. "It's the bloody drain," said Byam. "It's hogged, you know. I doubt if there's more than about half an inch to overflow. Take the rest of the night for this lot to get away. What we need is a pump..."

"What we don't have is a pump. We could bail it out," I said dubiously.

'It' was pretty unattractive. Mostly bathwater, it has to be said, but neither of us deluded ourselves – below this innocuous foot or so slumbered matter infinitely less recreative. I ran to the Colonel's potting shed and came back with two buckets and a galvanised dustbin and, as an afterthought, a length of rope, blessing the Colonel's meticulous arrangements. It would have taken half an hour so to equip myself at 14, The Pottergate. For five minutes or so, we bailed and emptied into the dustbin, and taking a handle each, ran and emptied it into the ditch. It was incredibly hard work. The water rose as fast as we emptied it.

"We'll never get anything done like this," said Byam, "What we need to do is sink a dustbin into the er... ordure, lift it out, carry it, empty it and come back for another one. Do that three or four times and we've solved the problem."

"But how do we sink the dustbin? What do we use for a weight?"

"Not what," said Byam, "Who. You stand in the dustbin, it sinks, fills up, we pull it out and Bob's your Uncle."

I pondered this hideous proposition for a few seconds. We toss for it," I said. "The loser goes into the dustbin."

As one man we took off our trousers and hung them side by side on the sheltering apple tree.

"My dear chap!" came the Colonel's voice from behind us. "My dear chap! You don't have to do this!"

"Our blood is up!" I said.

"So's the water level," said Byam.

"I can't tell you how grateful I am, but, really, I mean, your suit!" The Colonel was deeply distressed. "Brought you these. It was the least I could do." He handed each in turn a half pint glass which seemed to be over half full of whisky. "Are you sure there's nothing I can do? How can I help? I say, what about your clothes? Tell you what! You know where my room is – I'll put some things out for you. Can't... er." He waved an explanatory hand towards the tree from which Byam's suit had slid into the mud and, as we watched, mine followed it.

We dropped the dustbin with a solid splash into the mephitic interior of the tank, we passed a rope round its handles and gingerly I stood in it. With hideous stealth, it sank below me and with nauseating relish it filled to the brim with, I hardly like to think, what. With cracking shoulders, Byam and I hauled it out again and, slipping through the mud, ran once more to empty it in the ditch and repeated the process once, twice, three times and, miraculously, heard it grind on the solid concrete base so many feet below. I peeled off my shirt and mopped my brow. After a glance down at himself,

Byam followed and we stood there in our pants, repulsive and triumphant.

"If I know anything about North Suffolk," said Byam, "we could probably hire ourselves out doing this. No wedding complete without us when the word gets round!"

"I think this wedding will have to be complete without us, this time," I said.

Of course, in perfect order, neatly encircling a hose reel and securely fastened to a stand pipe, there was, by the back door, a garden hose. We remembered the Colonel's offer of a change of clothing, threw down the last of the Colonel's scotch, tossed our socks and pants to join the sorrowful heap under the apple tree and hosed each other down.

"Let's go and find the Colonel's clothes," I said when this icy operation was complete and, shivering, we ran to the house. We banged the back door open and fell into the kitchen – and into a scene from a painting by Breughel. We had forgotten the dinner ladies. The room was packed with large, pink, steamy women and their slim teenage messengers. Our precipitate arrival created an appreciative uproar.

"Cor! Luvly!" they said.

"Come to help have you?" said one, offering a pinny.

"No – I know who these are! They're the hunkogrammes! I've heard of them! You should hear what they got up to at Tilly's wedding! And they sing as well! Go on, then lads – give us one!"

I knew just how Susannah felt when viewed by the elders. We snatched up teatowels – Byam's said 'Suffolk Scanner Appeal' and mine, 'Save The Whale'. In their different ways, appropriate, I thought, as, inadequately robed in these, we fled up the stairs.

In the Colonel's room we found, laid out with his customary efficiency and order, two pairs of Welsh natural wool socks, two pairs of highly polished brown brogues, two pairs of voluminous aertex pants, two pairs of grey flannel trousers, two checked shirts, two cable knit jerseys, two ties (one regimental, the other Old Rugbeian) and two tweed jackets.

"We look like Tweedledum and Tweedledee," said Byam disgustedly surveying ourselves in a glass.

"You look more like Tweedledum than I do," I said, "Your trousers are too short."

When, having received a round of applause from the kitchen, we made our way over to the barn, we found Claire and Gentian, their legs tucked under them, seated companionably chatting on a straw bale.

"Darling!" said Claire when we came in view, "What *do* you look like!"

"Darling!" exclaimed Gentian, "You look wonderful! If only Daddy could see you now! All right – I will! Couldn't pass up a man who looked like that!"

"Oh, Byam," said Claire with the tear with which she greets any matrimonial arrangement, however preliminary, sparkling in her eye, "How lovely!"

A good deal of kissing followed. Claire kissed Byam, Gentian and Claire kissed me, Byam and I, the Heavenly Old Rugbeian Twins, shook hands in a manly sort of way. The Colonel hurried over, his torrent of thanks turning into a torrent of congratulations as he understood the situation. The group broke into the Dashing White Sergeant and the Colonel gathered up Gentian and Claire and plunged into the fray. After a little search, Byam and I found Iris and followed them.

"What's Daddy going to say?" I asked Byam over her head.

"Yeah, that's what I ask," said Byam. "In fact, in many ways, this is rather like the Waterloo Ball – calm before the storm, don't you know!"

"On with the dance, let joy be unconfined.
No sleep till dawn, when Youth and Pleasure meet,
To chase the glowing hours with flying feet," said Iris, surprisingly.

Chapter Nine

The Little Box.

Because Sir Hastings was the contemporary of the Lords and Ladies filling the topmost echelons of the National Trust and because he had been at school with such few of these to whom he was not related, he had always done a good deal of work for the National Trust, both in East Anglia and elsewhere. Mercifully, during his extended absence, enquiries from this quarter were very few and these were neatly fielded by Ron from his encyclopaedic memory of "what we did last time".

Our first autumn at Lavenham was an exceptionally wet one. Rain fell in torrents, torrents were followed by gales, tarpaulins blew off roofs and water rose in cellars as it never had before. On one such day when, every time I looked out of the window, it seemed that rain could get no heavier, it redoubled its maniacal and mindless persistence, I found Ron hunched like a small moulting parrot and blowing his nose dolefully into a spotted handkerchief.

"For God's sake, Ron! Go home! You don't have to stay here!" I looked at the neat list pinned to his wall. "You've got nothing today or tomorrow, then it's the weekend. Go home, have a bath, find a good book, go to bed!"

Ron shook his head. "Can't. Just had a call from the N.T. Felthorpe Hall." He scrabbled in the open file on the desk before him and produced the National Trust guide to Felthorpe Hall. "Main staircase. I've just been looking up Sir H's quinquennial. Where are we now? Ah yes, here we are -

'The condition of the main staircase has been mentioned in previous reports and its stability is now a matter of concern. A newel stair with four quarter space landings, its strength is dependent on the support each flight derives from the flight below. Provided tenons are sound, joints are tight and dowels hold their ground, the system is an adequate one but there is now reason to suspect that the visible distortion within this staircase has increased during the past five year period and the suspicion must now be that this is due to more than shrinkage and old age.

'I would suggest that where shrinkage gaps are to be seen, e.g. at junctions between newels and strings, small hardwood wedges be lightly inserted and, if the distortion referred to increases, these wedges will fall. Should this happen, further structural investigation would appear to be imperative.'

"Well it looks as though Sir H's little wedges have fallen out. The house is closed to the public but they've got a series of Christmas concerts it seems. One thing after another! So they ring me up – 'Is this staircase safe?' What am I supposed to say? Yes? No? So what *do* I say? 'Leave it to us. We'll come up and have a look.' He blew his nose dolorously once more, pushed his spectacles up onto his forehead and wiped his pink eyes.

"Rubbish, Ron. Either leave it until next week, or, if there's a panic on, I'll go for you. Why not? I don't think you'll make much sense in your present condition."

Ron blinked and shivered for a minute or two. "I've laid the builders on to get a few boards up for us. Bell & Son. Good firm. They've done all our work there. Johnny Bell will be there at half past two with a chippy. You sure that's all right ... ? "

"Sure! I've never been there .. Don't even know where it is but give me the file and I'll think of something. Where is it incidentally?"

"North Norfolk," said Ron apologetically.

Two and a half hours later, I swished my way, bouncing through the puddles in a haze of falling leaves up the long drive to Felthorpe Hall. Norfolk isn't Suffolk and that's a fact. The skies are wider, the building flints are bigger, the distances greater, and the cry of the wheeling plover more forlorn. Only fifty miles away from Lavenham, but Felthorpe Hall could never have been in Suffolk.

The front door was wide and welcoming, its brick dressings satisfyingly good-hearted and the lowering sun reflected from its many windows spoke of ancient warmth, but, 'Keep off! Go away!' said the house to me. 'Deus tute me spectas' said a stone inscription in the parapet. 'Thou, Lord, seeest me.' All too likely, I thought.

Mr. Bell, duly accompanied by his carpenter, greeted me in the hallway from which the fine newel stair climbed its way to a dim upper floor. I needn't have come, really. Mr. Bell and his carpenter were perfectly capable of taking up a few boards, dismantling a few stair treads and, indeed, diagnosing the problem and solving it. The Architect is very often the third wheel on the bicycle. This was one of those occasions.

"Didn't like to start until you got here Mr.... er... Thought if we took up two treads here and a floor board on the landing and perhaps the riser off the step up into the pass door, we ought to see what we're up to." I was about to say 'Nails must be cut and punched ...' but, almost before I could speak, the carpenter had slipped a hacksaw under the first stair tread and had started to cut the nails which held it in place.

When you take up ancient floor boarding or take down ancient panelling for that matter, or, as in this case, interfere with the structure of a staircase, it is impossible to extract the nails. These are blacksmith's nails and the very act of driving them into solid oak converts them from a straight, sharp spike, into something more like a corkscrew. Years of footsteps have worn the nail head away and years of polish have made it impossible to insert any sort of tool to extract the nail, even if it were possible to do so without splitting the board. Accordingly, it is necessary to cut the nail and punch it out from the back and subsequently to replace it with a new black iron blacksmith's nail.

In fact, when the nails were cut, the distortion in the staircase gave just enough tolerance to slip the stairtreads out of the strings without too much trouble and the risers followed with no more difficulty. We knelt together on the stairs and peered into the cavity which we had created. I held the torch while Johnny Bell felt within.

"The carriage has gone," he said. "It's supposed to be birdsmouthed under the trimmer and ..." feeling along the wall, "the wall string's gone in the same place."

I reached into the hole, broke off a section of timber and brought it out to the light.

"Death watch beetle," I said.

"How do you know?" said a voice from behind us.

I turned to confront a tall, stooping, bird-like figure peering over our shoulders. He reminded me at once of one of the bony herons I had seen on arrival, hunched at the edge of the lake. This was Nicholas Wemyss, the Curator, and introductions and explanations followed.

"How do you know?" he said again.

"If the flight holes are big enough to let you poke a match head into them, it's death watch beetle. If they're only big enough for a pin, it's woodworm – furniture beetle that is," I said, as I had been taught.

"Ah!" replied Nicholas looking impressed, "Now I really appreciate a complicated technical explanation! I shall remember that! But, Jack, is this serious? Should we do something about it? Does it mean the stairs are unsafe?

With practised authority, Johnny Bell said, "Well, it shouldn't be left. Death watch beetle is never a joke. Some of the bore dust," – he held out a sample in the palm of his hand – "is quite fresh and, no, it probably isn't quite safe. The newel is strutted by the outer string, that's really all that's holding the staircase up."

"We probably haven't seen all of it," I said. "If the other trimmer is in the same condition, then I'm afraid we really have got a problem. Let's see if we can take a board up on the quarter landing. That ought to tell us something"

Once more the hacksaw blade disappeared under the stair nosing and, one by one, the ancient nails were snipped through. The first mighty board came loose. Loose for the first time, I thought, since some ancient carpenter had tapped it into place three hundred years before. The carpenter waggled it to and fro, gingerly inserted the end of a nail bar and prised it upwards.

"I can't move it," he said in surprise. "It's stuck! There's something under there!" He inserted the end of a two foot rule. "Yes, something under there. That wholly bind when I try to lift it." He stepped back, scratching his head in puzzlement.

"Try the next one," said Johnny Bell and the process was repeated. With difficulty this time, because although it was possible to move the board an inch or so, it was difficult to feel for the nails. The shadows lengthened and the dim directional spotlight provided with such care by the National Trust hardly gave us enough light to work by. Johnny looked at his watch.

"We shall have to come back to this tomorrow," he said.

"I'll have to ring the Trust and tell them what we've found and what we're up to," I said to Nicholas.

"Mark Roberts is coming over tomorrow anyway," he told me and, as we spoke, the second board yielded to the carpenter's gentle persuasion and as he held it up Johnny Bell and I slipped our fingers beneath and lifted it out together.

With this obstruction gone, the first board came easily. It was very heavy. It was as much as the two of us could lift and, as it came from its ancient seating,

"Corst, blast!" said the carpenter, "There's a little old box fastened up to the bottom of that!"

"Little old box, nothing," said Nicholas. "It's a little old coffin!"

And it was. There was no mistaking it. The profile of a coffin lid is in some way branded on the memory. The eternal symbol of death and dissolution, an object of reasonless fear buried in the forgotten country memories of us all. It was tiny; not above two feet long. A whiff of profound grief and misery briefly embraced us all as the darkness became more profound, the thunderous rain began to fall again and the damp chill of the day sharpened to an icy coldness.

The carpenter ran a knowledgeable hand over the small structure. Of the four of us he was the least moved by this strange discovery. "Must have made hundreds of coffins in his time," I thought and, as though reading me, he said, absently caressing the joints with a craggy thumb,

"Oak boards. Nicely made. That's been here for a tidy while. That went in when they built the staircase. That were tacked up from below, look." He slipped the point of a chisel under the rim of the coffin and pressed upwards against the covering board. "Lift it off?"

What had we expected? Gold and silver? The lost infant heir of the Easton family – pathetic remains in a tattered winding sheet? What, in fact, we found was – nothing. The coffin might have been placed there yesterday. There was even a scatter of almost fresh sawdust.

"Well, I never saw the like of that!" said Johnny Bell, amazed. "What do you want done? Leave it till tomorrow, I suppose and then we'll get some more opened up and we'll be able to see how far we have to go. How soon can you get down tomorrow?"

In the end, after a good deal of telephoning and explaining, I was glad enough to accept to stay the night, and glad indeed to avoid two hours motoring back to Lavenham that night and two hours back again at dawn the next day.

"Not coming back tonight?" said Claire derisively over the telephone. "Found a nice milk maid in rural Norfolk have you?"

I explained my romantic circumstances which left her much intrigued.

Diana Wemyss, the curator's wife was no less intrigued. They were a bright pair and we easily settled for alternately frivolous and serious speculation towards any possible explanation for the mysterious reappearance of that strange little box.

At last, with dinner only half an hour away, Nicholas Wemyss invited me to come round with him as he 'put the house to bed'.

"This is the worst part of this job. It takes ages! Doors to lock. Alarms to set... Used to frighten me to death. I hardly dared to go out of my bedroom when we first got here in case I inadvertently summoned the police or the fire brigade or even set the place on fire by pressing the wrong button. I'm getting better at it now but it still takes about half an hour."

We wandered down through the dark house, our progress much delayed by Nicholas's discursions as we passed one beautiful thing after another. Pausing finally in the gallery which encircled the staircase at first floor level, he drew attention to a portrait. A harsh white face in a black periwig. He lifted the shade from a table lamp and held it upwards. A diamond ring on a thin white hand, a bunch of lace, lidded eyes, a clever face, a voluptuous face.

"William Easton," he said. "Not that that means much – they were all called William. It's very confusing. This is 'Wicked Easton', though I'm not quite sure why. He fought for the king at the battle of Worcester when he was eighteen and did all the proper things like escaping disguised as a lackey. I don't think he actually hid in an oak tree, but he did get away to Holland in a fishing boat from not far from here. Lots of girlfriends but he never married and died when he was forty. That was when the estate passed to the Lowndes."

We made a brief excursion into the library. "I always look very carefully in here. One of the troubles with walking round National Trust houses, of course, is that you can't sit on any of the chairs. People get very foot sore. We made a sort of reading room here where people could rest their feet for a minute or two if they wanted to. Came in here one evening and found someone asleep in one of the chairs! He'd got locked in. Gave me the fright of my life! I though I'd discovered the ghost of Felthorpe Hall! There isn't one," he added reassuringly.

Locking doors and turning out lights behind us, we returned to the landing.

"Hello? Wait a minute!" I said. "There's somebody downstairs."

"Can't be," said Nicholas comfortably. "There's nobody in the house except ourselves."

"Sorry. For a moment I thought I saw someone under the stairs. Where does that door lead to?"

"Doesn't lead anywhere. It's been blocked for over a hundred years."

"Perhaps it was the moon ..."

"Well now, that really would be a miracle! No moon through all this cloud." And we returned to the cheerful, candlelit dining room under the roof.

Chapter Ten

The Little Box (Part Two).

Many hours later and equipped with a toothbrush, a disposable razor and a pair of Nicholas's pyjamas, I was shown to a small spare room on the floor below.

"Hope you'll be all right in here? There's a little sort of wash place through that door over there. We'd better aim for eight o'clock breakfast. Suit you? Well, sleep well!"

The little room in which I found myself, in some complicated way that I hadn't worked out, seemed to form a mezzanine stage in the front porch and, in consequence, three out of its four walls were of glass. It had been a long day and I had hardly been able to keep my eyes open for the last hour or so, but, as soon as I reached this little room, I realised that I was in for a sleepless night. My mind went into unwelcome overdrive and a blend of disconnected calculations began to flood through. Schemes for the repair of the stairs were uppermost but speculation as to the possible history of the little box followed close behind. Telephone calls that I should have made from the office jostled these things for my attention.

It was a welcoming room, the bed comfortable, the selection of bedside reading promising, the curtains were thick but sleep eluded me. I turned on the light and then turned it off again. I got out of bed, drew the curtains and looked out across the park. The moon appeared briefly through a rent in the cloud and a flight of mallard whipped swiftly across this luminous patch. Memories of Antony and Cleopatra, my 'A' level text, returned to me -

"And there is nothing left remarkable beneath the visiting moon".

Not so sure about that!

I turned disconsolately back to bed and my eye was caught by an armorial cartouche over the door – 'Thou, God, see'st me', the Easton motto once more. Determinedly I drew the 'Pick Of Punch' from the bookcase and, with the sense of sin that always descends on me when I smoke upstairs (strictly forbidden by my father and, no doubt, by the National Trust also) I lit a cigarette. An unsatisfactory proceeding. I stubbed it out and climbed back into bed. Instantly the unwelcome message came to me that I had to have a pee. Cursing and swearing and feeling very sorry for myself, I made my reluctant way onto the landing and, failing to find the light switch, proceeded by the guidance of my bedside light to the head of the stairs and on to the bathroom. On my return I was, still more reluctantly, drawn to peer down into the darkness below.

A door opened and shut and a dim figure two floors below slipped under the stairs and into the unseen hallway.

"There *is* somebody down there! I knew it! Somebody *has* got locked into the house. But surely the whole place is covered with movement detectors? Who the hell's that?"

My speculation was answered by a sigh from below and an indistinguishable gabble of words in a female voice. The gabble of words terminated in a rack of sobbing and I was much afraid.

A shaft of light broke from a suddenly opened door on the floor above and the Wemyss peered down over the balustrade.

"Jack?"

"Yes?"

"Did you hear that?"

"Yes. There *is* somebody down there. I thought there was."

"Can't be," said Nicholas. "Can't be."

"But I heard them!"

"Not them – her." Diana's voice.

They hurried down the stairs and joined me. I was very glad of their warmth and nearness. The house was desperately cold.

"We heard someone on the stairs," they said.

"That was me going to the loo."

"No, before that. Did it wake you up?"

"No, I wasn't asleep. But I did see someone just now. And there – look there!"

Nicholas, lucky man, gathered his wife to him and the tail of a shaft of passing moonlight seemed again to illuminate a white figure and, once again, that mutter of pathetic sobbing.

"Come on, Jack," said Nicholas. "Let's go and look at this!"

"You're not leaving me up here all by myself," said Diana firmly.

But that was all we saw that night. We turned on all the lights, we circumvented the burglar alarms, we searched the staircase and its landing. We even looked, ridiculously, into the little box. Nothing. No one. No sound.

"If I might make rather a folksy suggestion," I said, "would we like a cup of tea?"

"Now, that's what I really appreciate," said Nicholas, with an attempt at lightness. "'The sheeted dead did squeak and gibber in the Roman streets' and the Englishman calls for a cup of tea!"

"Just shut up, Nicholas! Shut up!" said Diana with unexpected venom. Pale faced, she glanced round, her dark eyes wide with fear.

There was a hiss, a whirr and a metallic click as we mounted the stairs and, after a moment of aged hestitation, an ancient clock struck one.

"What did the carpenter say?" asked Diana when we sat down in the kitchen, fragrant cups of Earl Grey clutched in shaking hands. "That the coffin must have been there when the staircase was built?

When was that? 1660? Then perhaps Mr. Stillingfleet can help us!"

"Mr. Stillingfleet?" I asked, "Who's he?"

"Was. Hugo Benedict Stillingfleet. He was tutor to the little Easton boys."

"Wicked Easton?"

"Yes, Wicked William and his brother Charles. And then he was domestic chaplain and finally steward. He lived here for about fifty years and kept the most wonderful account books. More like a diary than the usual account book. Every single farthing that got spent, Stillingfleet recorded it. Everybody who came or went he recorded as well. He was certainly here when the staircase was built because I remember reading his final calculation of the cost – he was horrified that it had cost so much – about £480 I think. All the men who worked on it are named and the wages they were paid. He made a note of anyone who was in the employ of the family and what they earned. He even recorded family journeys and who came to stay, practically what they had for breakfast! He must have been a wonderful man. He wrote a lot of poetry and, as a young man, he'd been a friend of Edmund Waller. There are volumes of manuscript poems downstairs, all very classical -

'When I look in Chloe's eyes,
Summer flowers and summer skies .....'

"All that sort of thing. If anything funny happened when the staircase was being built, I'll bet Stillingfleet knew about it and if he knew about it, he recorded it! It was his way. Nick – go and get Stillingfleet and let's have a look!"

"I'm not getting Stillingfleet at this time of night! It weighs about three tons for a start and to go on with – I don't want to unlock the library. It'll keep till the morning."

After a while, I began to drowse again and the sleep that had so long eluded me began to return until at last I said,

"That coffin. We moved it. Did we release something? Something very small. Something very sad. Did we call back somebody? Somebody who is distraught at the disturbance?"

"We'll ask Stillingfleet in the morning," said Nicholas and we finally went to bed.

I didn't get away from Felthorpe until the early afternoon, but, in the time, we had fully revealed the state of the damage which was not more extensive than we had at first supposed, agreed a detail for its repair, worked out a possible cost and obtained the authority of the National Trust to proceed. I had hardly seen Diana during the course of the morning. Both she and Nicholas were in their sitting room buried in Stillingfleet's tome and when we parted we agreed to meet in one week's time to inspect the finished repair.

The little box stood in neglect, propped in the corner of the landing as I made my way down the stairs and out through the front door.

I sat in my car for a few moments and, on impulse, returned to the staircase and picked up the coffin. I took it into the library and placed it carefully on the long central table and left a note by it for Nicholas, assuring him that he hadn't got a poltergeist – I had moved the coffin there myself for safe keeping. I didn't want it to end up on a builder's bonfire.

A week later I returned. Bell & Son had done a beautiful job and had only delayed its final completion so that I could pass it, which I gladly did.

Diana and Nicholas were both very subdued. "We've had terrible nights," they said, "and we've got a lot to tell you."

They stood impatiently by while I did my site inspection before leading me into the library. The table was covered with pages of notes. With hardly suppressed excitement, but striving to maintain the air of a company secretary reading a dull minute to an assembled boardroom, Diana went straight into the result of her researches.

"This is 1660," said Diana, one finger on her notes and turning the ponderous pages of the bound Stillingfleet papers with the other hand. "Here's the boss telling him to get estimates – 'Ye new westerne stair' – but it seems they forgot about it for a year because it wasn't till 1661 that Jas. Holbrooke, Master Carpenter, rides out from Norwich to talk about it seriously. And look, here's his estimate – £482.9.2d Expensive!"

"V.A.T. exclusive though, no doubt," I said automatically.

"Yes, I expect so. And here we are 1662. A lot of comings and goings. The family were here for nearly all of that year. Lots of company. – 'My Lord Southwold and his Lady with numerous train.' They ate them out of house and home it would seem. The household bills went up alarmingly in 1662! ... John Chandler and his brother Will, taken up for pilfering at the Lammas fair and the good Stillingfleet goes over to the Assizes to plead for them. Successfully, obviously, because they were back on the payroll the next month. And here's one Jayne Maston (or Marston, he spells it either way)."

"Probably pronounced Marston whichever way you spell it," put in Nick.

"Yes, Jayne Marston – 'Miss Comfort's abigail'. Lady's maid. Quite posh. Comes down from London. This is still in January so it was quite a busy month. Now why did Jayne Marston come down from London without Miss Comfort, I wonder?"

Something in her tone led me to say, "Important? Is she important?"

"Well, wait and see," and she resumed. "There are a surprising number of references to her – 'Ye sorrowful Jayne' (Must be the same

Jayne, there are no others mentioned) and again – 'That forlorn wretch. That sweet slut in her sorrow.' Something wrong there, don't you agree? And then, of course, the staircase gets under way. An apprentice steals a length of lead pipe and gets a 'right goode thrashing' for his pains."

"Could happen to anyone," I said.

"He'd get a hundred hours community service now, I suppose," said Nicholas.

".... And then in about April they start getting ready for a party... seems to be a belated celebration of the restoration of King Charles the Second – the Eastons were all stout monarchists. They probably wanted to make their mark on Norfolk society, now that society had swung round to their way of thinking again ... Then in June two or three things happen – 'Did wait on Master William under God's guidance and besought him to remember his Creator in the days of his youth, when the evil days come not.' "

"Did he? Remember his Creator, I mean?"

"It doesn't say but one rather infers *not* and then – dismay and disaster – on the fifteenth of June – 'To me at dawn this day comes the swanward early. Jayne Maston, God receive her, found drowned in ye lake.'"

Diana turned to me with big eyes. "And she's not in the burial register! She's not buried in the churchyard!"

"Suicide?"

"Well it looks like it doesn't it? And then William disappears."

"Disappears?"

"Yes – 'raging to London' that's all – 'raging to London', leaving poor old Stillingfleet to unscramble the party."

"And the staircase?"

"Finished, because here ... about a week before ... 'Thanks be to God!' Then – and this is perhaps where the fun starts – 'Twas as though the Devil himself wailed about the house this night and these seven nights past, God bless us all'."

"Is that what it's been like?"

"Perhaps not quite like that – sobs rather than wails – but going on and on. Just the same for Stillingfleet. At the end of every day he wrote just two words ... 'No change' until we get to 'All day working in pursuit of my resolve'."

"Working? Working at what, I wonder?"

"Well, in addition to all his other accomplishments, Mr. Stillingfleet was a carpenter and a turner and he made tables and chairs and gates and he was a bit of a scientist too. He had a workshop. We think it was the little room at the end of the stillroom passage."

I pretended I knew what she meant. " 'All day working in pursuit of my resolve'? Working at what, do you think? Coffin?" "Yes, that's what we think. It's a long shot and we shall never know, but, listen – Jayne Maston is sent down to the country estate from London without her mistress. Pregnant?"

"Is that consistent? Is that what they would have done in those days? Wouldn't she just have been turned out of the house?"

"I don't think so – not then. This wasn't the Protectorate, you know. This was the Restoration. Cavalier politics and Cavalier morality. Cavalier kindness if you like. The Eastons were notable for their large-heartedness. But suppose I'm right. Suppose Jayne Maston comes down to Norfolk because she's pregnant. Suppose Wicked William is the father. Suppose he comes down for the party and takes no notice of her or spurns her even and perhaps that was what Hugh Stillingfleet was begging him to remember, begging him to do something for the wretched girl. And then the baby arrives and is stillborn? Or dies perhaps?"

"Dies? How? And where?

"How? We don't know. And where? Well, I think something – God knows what – happened *on* the stairs. Let's just say the baby dies. There is no recorded death of an infant at this time ... Suppose the body just disappears ... Snatched away by William perhaps? Poor Jayne goes demented and follows her baby."

"Did she fall or was she pushed?" I asked.

"Let's give William the benefit of the doubt and say she fell ... well, threw herself into the lake, distracted because she didn't know what had happened to her baby ... No Christian burial ... no baptism even ... And then, you see, Stillingfleet makes a little coffin. What to do with it? I think, one night, as the staircase was nearly finished, he fixes the coffin under a floorboard, puts the floorboard down and says a burial service over it. It was the best he could do."

"Any more from the diary?"

"Only this, but significantly, – 'Under the hand of God, I pray, I finish my work and, all praise to Him, a quiet night at last.'"

We sat for a moment in silence and at last I said, "I bet that was it, or something very like that. Yes, it really does hang together. Something like that must have happened."

"What do we do now?"" said Nicholas.

"I think we put the coffin back again, or ask Johnny Bell to."

"Could you put the coffin back?" asked Diana.

"Yes, I think so."

"Say the burial service over it?" said Nicholas, embarrassed.

"I think it would be enough to say 'May he rest in peace' or something like that," said Diana.

" 'He' do you think?"

"Yes, I'm almost certain – no, I *am* certain it was 'he'."

We turned the board over and saw once more the outline of the little coffin. We laid it back in its place and, and, finding a bag of treenails on the stair, and borrowing a hammer from Nicholas, I tapped them back into position through the rim which the thoughtful Hugo Stillingfleet had left for this purpose. It wasn't difficult. The new nails slipped easily into the ancient holes and Nicholas and I with some struggle lifted the board and tapped it back into position. Once again, the new nails sank in easily. We stood back and looked at each other uncertainly.

"May he rest in peace and light perpetual shine upon him," said Diana quietly and clearly.

A few days later Ron – now more or less recovered from his cold and in reply to my question said, "No, not much in the post. Just a postcard from some girlfriend of yours in Norfolk."

He held it out to me. The message was short –

"All praise to Him, a quiet night at last. Diana."

Chapter Eleven

The Dusky Gent.

Heather wasn't much of a one for gadgetry and it was even some time before we were able to persuade her that we really needed a telephone each, but, once she got the idea, she began to warm up and even suggested the introduction of a small telephone exchange. It fell to Byam to arrange for this and soon, in addition to the exchange, a little box appeared on Byam's desk whereby his telephone could be set in conference mode and when we could not compel him to switch it off we heard both sides of his conversations.

On one particular day, a call came straight through to him and, to my irritation, I heard him, after a few moments reflection, select from his repertoire a voice from the Gulf States in which to reply.

"Oh, good morning, Sir. Here is Sir Hasting Munro office. Who is speaking please?"

There was a perceptible pause at the other end and Byam repeated his question. At last, a puzzled voice came back to us.

"Oh, good morning, Sir. Ismailia Property and Development Company here."

It might have been Byam's twin!

"Serve you bloody well right!" I said. "I've been expecting this to happen! Now what are you going to do?"

But Byam was undaunted. "Oh, Sir Hasting Munro no here."

Reading his mind, I was wondering whether he dared say 'Bismillah' or something of that sort. Before he could do so he was subjected to a flood of what I suppose was Arabic and at that point, looking as confused as I have ever seen him, he turned off the conference mike and we only heard one side of the ensuing conversation.

"Alexander here. Hemsley Castle? Know it well. Well, that sounds very interesting – no, we'd be delighted to deal with it – Sir Hastings will be away for a few more weeks I'm afraid but – let me see – yes, I think tomorrow can be arranged. At three fifteen? No problem. I'll probably bring my assistant, Mr. Simpson with me. Yes, I'll be looking forward to it too. Thank you very much Mr. .. er.." and he came away from the telephone beaming with relief.

"Well, well, well," he said, "this might be the big one! Hemsley Castle, eh? Quite a pile, one way or another. It seems we have a Mr. Al-Khalil from the State of D'Juddah. I'm very much in favour of oil-rich Arabs, anxious to restore ancient castles and I forsee plenty of timeless houris and invitations to confer with the Boss Man in a sun-drenched palace on the Persian Gulf. I'm glad I answered the telephone," he concluded with a certain amount of satisfaction.

"Hemsley Castle's alright," said Ron. "Used to belong to Sir George and Lady Mason. Shipping people. Left it, with a life interest for his brother, to the Nation. What did the Nation do? Flogged it off! Quite a scandal about it two or three years ago. What sort of a house? Well, it's not exactly a castle. Moated but no castle. Great big courtyard house. Timber framed. Nice. We did some roofing there, oh, it must have been twenty years ago."

Heather had been searching through a large atlas extracted from Sir Hastings' library. "It's a con," she said, "There's no such place as D'Juddah! It's one of your friends having you on!"

Byam came and looked over her shoulder and riffled through the atlas. "You're not likely to find it in an atlas printed in 1912!" he said disparagingly. And, turning a few pages, "French Equatorial Africa? Austro-Hungary? Blimey! In 1912 most of the oil states were part of the Turkish Empire!"

"I don't suppose it exists," said Heather once more, but she was wrong as we were to find.

Byam and I duly made our way to Ismailia House the following day for our appointment at 3.15. "3.15 indeed!" I said. "What sort of wally makes an appointment for 3.15?"

"It's humiliation therapy," said Byam eying the reception area which was decorated in black, white and orange and contained a very great deal of plant life with disfavour as secretarial persons, colour-matched to the general decor, clicked to and fro across the marble floor.

"I feel like a man in a perspective," muttered Byam, resentfully, as we sat side by side on a leather sofa on which it was impossible to do other than recline at full length or sit, uncomfortably perched, on the edge. "Humiliation therapy, that's what it is! Saladin strikes back.

It's their revenge for the centuries when the Raj held the Gorgeous East in fee!"

A quarter of an hour and a cup of coffee later (served in white and orange cups on black saucers) we followed a neat bum in a black skirt beneath a white shirt and an orange scarf round the neck into a lift. It only had two buttons and there was no physical sensation to tell you that the lift was moving at all until it delivered to the penthouse floor and, having passed through a small lobby in which an expressionless dusky person with a flower-power moustache was sitting in timeless contemplation of the lift door, to a room in which a middle aged lady was sitting under a contour map of the State of Djuddah at a desk the size of a ping-pong table. She was wearing a silky grey suit and an icy stare with which she kept us pinned to the long sofa in her domain. Having spent another ten minutes or so, in Byam's case reclining and in mine, perching, we were summoned by a flashing light over an inner door and ushered into the presence.

Grey white and black this time. There were four men in the room, two of whom introduced themselves as Mr. Maflak and Mr. El-Kader. A third, who sat on a chair by the door was not introduced and took no part in the ensuing conversation. Neither did the fourth who inscrutably and disconcertingly sat behind us in motionless silence. Mr. Maflak and Mr. El-Kader, however, took up the tale in a voluble cascade.

"Our Principal, Mr. Al-Khalil, has bought Hemsley Castle from your government for a good figure. We have friends," flash of alarmingly white teeth, "good friends, in important places you understand. They very pleased Mr. Al-Khalil put the house in order for them. Live in it as private house. We interview six ... seven architects and then we make our choice. Ok? We need full restoration and modernisation. If you will believe Mr. Alexander and Mr. ..er ... twenty five bedrooms and only four bathrooms! No central heating and no lift. Central courtyard has a brick floor. A brick floor! Mr. Al-Khalil will say marble, that's for certain! We shall want servant houses."

"Servant houses?" I asked. "With twenty five bedrooms?"

"Mr. Al-Khalil will not want servants in the house and he will want three, four guest suites."

I began to detest them quite cordially but, receiving a warning glance from Byam who had read the signs, I left the ensuing conversation to him. His detestation threshold is a good deal higher than mine.

After an hour or so, in which I had filled several pages of notes, and after an exchange of cordial handshakes in which the Silent One did not join, we left with a request that we would, within the coming twenty four hours quote them a fee.

As we stepped back into the lift, appropriately escorted,

"I wonder," I asked, "who were the other two?"

"Well, one of them I think was a bodyguard," said Byam. "Did I detect a bulge under the armpit of the Brooks Brothers suit revealing the presence of the standard issue Beretta? The sons of the Prophet are hardy and bold and quite unaccustomed to fear... but no one in his senses would interview a couple of architects without a little armed backup. The other, I think, was probably the boss man himself."

And, indeed, our escort shyly confirmed as much.

The next day Byam went by himself to look Hemsley Castle over and came back full of enthusiasm. "Beautiful house," he said. "Damn shame really. Doesn't need anything done to it as far as I can see. Bit shabby perhaps, but none the worse for that in my opinion. Courtyard's beautiful. Marble indeed! The park's very much part of the house. No way in this world that you could site "servant houses" all over it. I can see that we're going to have to educate these guys. And how on earth we quote an all in fee is more that I can imagine."

"Think of a number and then double it. Add the number you first thought of and double it again," said Ron.

And this is more or less what we did. We quoted a fee that, as Byam said, should enable Sir Hastings to lay in two years' supply of Vilar y Vilar. In this we were much assisted by a set of floor plans which Ron found somewhere. They were nostalgically sprinkled with such legends as – "Lady M.'s Sitting Room", "Silver Pantry", "Head House Maids" to say nothing of "The Saloon, the Dining Room, the Small Dining Room, the Still Room, the Estate Office" and so on.

We made a proposal, we drafted a Form of Agreement, we hedged it about with concealed ifs, buts and probables; we thought we'd done a good job. We didn't believe the other six or seven architects existed and we awaited a reply and waited and waited.

A month later there came a call from the talkative Mr. Maflak – "We really need to get on with this," he said, accusingly. "Mr. Al-Khalil thinks we've wasted enough time. He will be at the castle tomorrow. Will you meet him at ten fifteen?"

"Hmm," said Byam, "Ten fifteen's a bit awkward. Could you make it ten twenty?"

It was the first sign of revolt.

Our meeting with Mr. Al-Khalil, duly supported by Mr. Maflak and Mr. El-Kader, and not unaccompanied by other shadowy figures, was affability itself. He was tall, he was thin, he was elegant. He was expensively dressed. He had a pencil thin hairline moustache and looked rather like Don Ameche in his early days. No reference was made whatever to the month's interval that had passed during which we supposed, rightly as it turned out, that absolutely nothing had happened at all until the day came when Mr. Al-Khalil discovered that he had a morning, an afternoon, a day with nothing else to do.

We discussed, we drew, we designed, we calculated, we made a provisional forecast of various costs and we did a very great deal of agreeing. We had a pretty good lunch which had been sent down from Harrods. We left, shaking hands a considerable number of times with most of those present with instructions to proceed but with the proviso – "You wait until Mr. Maflak confirm and then we get on straight away. No problem."

Six weeks later, we thought it might be reasonable to ring and enquire whether we might expect a confirmation of our verbal instructions.

"Oh, just a little problem ... Mr. Al-Khalil still interviewing these architects and we wait until he has seen representatives of a big New York consortium. Perhaps you work in with them. We write to you. No hurry."

"Told you so," said Heather.

"Listen," said Byam, "We are very grateful for all you are doing for us and we realise that it is putting you to a great deal of trouble. We don't want you to be personally out of pocket over this because we know that you would have better things to do with your time. Of course, we always pay ten per cent of the gross fee for a valuable introduction of this sort, but we really think that you have gone a good deal further on our behalf than we could possibly have expected and you really must let us see that you are all right."

"Ah, my friend," said Mr. Maflak, "you do not have to do this!" But it was clear that our fumbling hand had at last found the right button and pressed it because within a very few days came instructions to proceed. Not in writing, of course, but we took the trouble to confirm all that had been said and got on with it.

We designed bathrooms, we discreetly sited soil pipes, we had a test on the sewage disposal unit, ("Nah Poo Squire I'm afraid"), we enlisted the help of the Local Planning Authority and had their permission to quote them as each time we headed off Mr. Al-Khalil's wilder ideas. We even managed to persuade him that a two storey house with attics did not require a lift. Hemsley Castle is well supplied with lodges of which only two at this time were occupied and of which it was felt that the remaining four would adequately supply the need for servant houses. Byam spent quite a lot of his weekends lunching with Mr. Al-Khalil and, by degrees, an agreed set of drawings, an agreed schedule of costs and the blessing of the Planning Authority, to say nothing of the Building Control Division were secured. We were almost ready to go out to tender but here our troubles began.

Firstly, Mr. Al-Khalil, whom we had never succeeded in contacting direct by telephone, his limited attention span exhausted, left for Gstaad and an agreement from Ismailia House of our proposed tender list became the subject of endless, pointless telephone calls.

"Mr. Al-Khalil say that there is a very good man in the village who will do all the work at half the price. He want you to negotiate with him. OK?"

"No, not OK!" said Byam crossly, "You can't hand a job of this size to a bloke who's got one ladder, one motor bike and side car and perhaps half a paint brush! A firm of that sort would take about twenty years to do a million pounds worth of work."

"Oh, Mr. Alexander, Mr. Al-Khalil not pleased. The man came when we had the roof leak. He came on a Saturday. He say he can do it. No problem. And we have Mr. René de Saint Cirq who is great, oh very great, and he will do the kitchen. Mr. Al-Khalil was very impressed, oh yes, very impressed with his kitchens at Gentilly."

"But," said Byam in a voice as near to a bleat as I had ever heard him utter, "we have already designed the kitchen!"

"Oh, yes, very good, but Mr. Al-Khalil say no good enough."

This, if we had had eyes to see, was really the beginning of the end. Our lives were rendered almost intolerable by the procession of experts who now began to appear. There was Mr. Giudecci, "from the Palazzo Farnese, very great expert on wall paintings" whom I was only just in time to prevent from scrubbing down the Elizabethan wall paintings in the green bedroom with a packet of sugar soap and a Brillo pad.

There was a wretched man called Markham who had been engaged to lay out a nine hole golf course ("we just take down two, three trees"). There was an unbroken procession of interior decorators, some having nationally if not internationally known names, (two indeed from New York). One or two from neighbouring villages, some cynical, some starry-eyed, all to be disappointed. The foolish put a lot of time into the house. The wise awaited the written instructions that never came.

"What this must be costing them!" said Byam. "I suppose all these guys get paid?"

"Why should you suppose that? *We* don't get paid."

"Oh yes, we do," said Ron. "Heather's been sending them monthly accounts ever since we started! Heather!" he shouted, "What do Ali Baba and the Forty Thieves owe us now? ... There – told you so, only £250 on the ledger for last month. Oh no, we've been billing 'em. Don't you worry! Saw them coming a mile off! I don't mind Pharaoh having his revenge if that's what he wants, but I made sure he didn't have it at our expense!"

"Good God!" said Byam, "How much have you billed them so far?"

"Oh, I dunno," said Ron, "Have to look it up."

We did look it up.

"Another six months at this rate," I commented, "and there won't be any money left at all. And we haven't laid a brick or wielded a paint brush or accepted a tender! I'll tell you what it is, you know ... You and I, we were brought up in the shadow of Roman law, Norman business morality and here we are, I guess, in a back street in the Souk!"

"Yes, whatever happened to Arabs?" mused Byam, "Unsurpassed architecturally, mathematicians, astronomers, poets, engineers. But now? Never seem to want to get on with anything."

And in this, for a short while, it seemed that he was right. With Mr. Al-Khalil in Gstaad, and no reasonable prospect of extracting any instructions from Mr. Maflak or Mr. El-Khader on which we could act, we forgot about Hemsley Castle and left it contemplating its reflection in the moat in dreamy neglect.

But about a month after the conversation I have just described, curiosity overcame us and, hearing that Mr. Maflak was to be at the castle, Byam made an appointment from which he came back fuming with rage.

"Do you know what I found? The billiard room has been fitted out from end to end with fluorescent lighting, half a dozen drawing boards manned by half a dozen doe-eyed Bedouin. Couple of plan chests, fax machine, computer, all the trimmings!"

"But what were they doing?"

"Well, as far as I could see," said Byam grimly, "they were tracing off our drawings and retitling them. Mr. El-Khader was installed in what used to be called the Steward's office, large executive style desk, about four telephones, portrait of the Ruler, you've never seen anything like it! 'Oh,' said Mr. El-Khader, 'Now working here as project manager. We got our own people now. Mr. Al-Khalil, he said we got to get some action so we got our own people.'

"And that wasn't all! I went upstairs. The whole bloody place was swarming with painters. Blow lamps! Paint stripper, scrapers, emulsion in various shades – knicker pink in the Print Room if you can believe it! And do you remember a line of eighteenth century leather fire buckets in the Gun Room passage? Found them in the bloody skip! (It's all right I've rescued them!) 'Updating the fire precautions are we?' I said, but they didn't get the point.

"And the electrical services! Cables running up and down the panelling! There was a telephone wire inserted through a hole casually drilled in a window frame. They've put ranks of gilt standard lamps of the nastiest possible sort in the Saloon..." His voice trailed away miserably.

"What on earth did you say?"

"Well, old boy, I hope you won't mind about this but I said to Maflak, I said, 'What are you doing on Monday?'

"Monday? What should I be doing on Monday?'

"So I said to him, 'I'll tell you what you're doing old chap, you're finding another architect!' Good exit line, I think you'll agree, and I packed my tents, mounted my camel and rode away into the sunset. Though, for one hideous moment, I almost blew my exit! You may recall that my car is in dock. You may even recall that I have on loan from Cherry Hinton Motors a mark 1 Cortina. Excellent car in many ways but a bastard to start."

I did indeed recall this fact and without much difficulty because Ron and I had spent quite a lot of time over the past few days pushing Byam in his pea green Cortina up and down the High Street to get it started.

"An anxious moment! Figure to yourself the humiliation had I been constrained after my dramatic exit to go back and recruit some dusky ones to push me down the drive. But Allah the All Merciful was on my side for once and for perhaps the first time in its fifteen year old career the All Green One started first go! Just about the only good moment in a bad day."

"But what did they say?"

"They didn't say much. In fact, now I come to look back on it, I don't believe they said anything and, mortifying as it may seem, I think they were only too glad to see the back of me. I hope you don't mind?"

"Mind? No! I'm only too relieved!"

And that was almost the end of Hemsley Castle as far as we were concerned. And though, for quite a long time thereafter, the telephone rang at intervals and excited voices from other architects, some of whom we knew, some of whom we didn't know, each saying that they had been appointed to act in the matter of Hemsley Castle and was that all right as far as we were concerned? None of them lasted. Contractors came and went; the mass of name boards at the gate got larger and smaller. One by one, as we heard, the doe-eyed Bedouin in the drawing office drifted away; painters, plumbers and landscape gardeners faded away likewise and nothing further was heard from Mr. Al-Khalil.

One evening, Byam and I found ourselves driving home through Hemsley and slipped off the road to visit the Castle which was deserted, silent and shuttered but for what seemed to be a forty watt bulb seen through a small window near the kitchen. Beautiful house where, for five hundred years, men had lived and loved, been born and died, married and given in marriage, set off for the war and come back again, was deserted. With the advance of reeds in the moat, the swans had gone away and the only sound was the occasional peep from a moor hen as it sculled to and fro under the Gothic bridge.

As we stood by the car, watching through the dusk, the low sun came momentarily out from behind a cloud and for a second the whole of the west front was illuminated as though by lamp light from within and as though the house was, once more, dressed overall for a hunt ball or a coming-of-age. But as we watched, the sun sank behind a bank of cloud and the momentary illusion was no more.

"Dans le grand parc solitaire et glacé,

Deux ombres spectrales évoquent le passé..." said Byam sententiously.

"I wonder where Monsieur got his accent français si parfait?"

"My mother was born in Paris. I sometimes think it accounts for my panache, my élan, my joie de vivre, to say nothing of my espièglerie."

"Mm... It might also account for your minauderie."

"Minauderie?"

"Mincing ways, I think, or something of that sort. Was your mother really born in Paris?"

"Not exactly. She was born in the shadow of the Château de Brotonne, just to the west... " he finished mysteriously, then added with smile, "Minauderie... I must remember the word. Didn't get us far with the Arabs though, did it?"

Chapter Twelve

Kight's Move.

"I am hoping over the next years to cut down my working hours to be able to travel and work less but more widely ..."

These had been Sir Hastings' words. For years he had been planning a major architectural work of which, as time went by, the size had increased but the scope had diminished. Originally to be titled "Colonial Architecture", it had been retitled "American Colonial Architecture" and was finally to emerge as "Early American Colonial Architecture" as his wide ranging mind and bubbling enthusiasm led him down one intriguing alley after another.

Devious as ever, and with a characteristic determination that his left hand should not know what his right hand doeth, he had told Byam and me that he would be away for a month. He had told Ron that he would be away for two months and he had told Heather that he would be away for three months. He was, in fact, away for ten months, two weeks and four days. We were able to follow his erratic flight across the southern United States from a series of postcards illustrating, as a rule, one noble antebellum mansion after another, usually embellished with a valueless news item – "Staying here for a few days. Wonderful weather" or "Had to dash across to see this! Worth the detour I think you'll agree!"

A few days after our twilight visit to Hemsley, I went back to the office one evening just before supper and was surprised to see light streaming, not only from the office, but from Sir Hastings' library as well. With curiosity I let myself in through the front door and was instantly greeted by a not-forgotten and instantly remembered voice from the half landing.

"Ah, my dear Alexander!" As neat, as dapper, as pink and cheerful as ever, Sir Hastings stood, rubbing his hands and beaming down with vague benevolence. "Ah, my dear Alexander! Come to burn some midnight oil? That's the way! Got to keep ahead of the game!"

I was quite surprisingly glad to see him. It wouldn't be true to say that we had missed him, but every job we had done, every client we had met, every line we had drawn had, as it had seemed, been under his benevolent eye and his jaunty personality had continued to pervade the house.

"Come in, come in and tell me all that's been happening."

Something in his tone inspired me to say, "I'd love to do that, but it's a very long story and – have you had dinner?"

Five minutes later, we were walking down to the Pottergate

together. I, wondering if there was going to be enough supper for three, Sir Hastings talking non stop.

"Show you all my sketches in the morning (or shall we go back and fetch them? No? You're probably right). Wonderful country, charming people! The hospitality! Spent six weeks with the Cabot-Vanderbilts. Couldn't do too much for me! (Had a bit of a job getting away to tell you the truth). Beautiful house – High Beeches. Drove me everywhere, waited on me hand and foot. Wonderful! And then Atlanta! Have you been to Atlanta? You should go. Perhaps we'll all go. Came back with a trunk full of notes. Publisher yapping at my heels. Goodness knows when I'll get through it all. You fellers may have to get by a bit longer without me. Been wondering whether 'Some Aspects of Early American Colonial Architecture' mightn't be a better title?

"So you bought number 14 did you? Ah! We should have seen this street before the warehouse was built! Perhaps the most outstanding row of timber framed houses in the world! And all swept away, my dear Alexander, all swept away...!"

I pushed the creaking door of number 14 open and ushered Sir Hastings up the steps ahead of me, hoping that Claire had not pursued a half expressed intention of washing her hair. She hadn't. Sir Hastings greeted her without any perceptible pause to indicate that he had changed gear,

"Mrs. Simpson! The wanderer returned you see! My Odyssey, completed, 'Quae regio in terris?' as you might say. Where haven't I been! I must tell you all about it! And how charming you've made this room! Delightful! Quite delightful!"

Momentarily astonished, Claire rallied, greeted Sir Hastings with considerable warmth, muttered to me that I was only to eat one chop and we settled Sir Hastings down in front of the fire.

He had spent six months in aeroplanes passing backwards and forwards across the United States, he had just crossed the Atlantic and travelled down from Heathrow laden with luggage to a cold and empty house and he was only a few months off his seventieth birthday but, hardly having drawn breath, between his arrival and his departure, he kept us talking and listening till after midnight and, of the two bottles we had consumed, I'll swear that Claire and I had not drunk more than half a bottle between us.

As he rose to depart, only slightly unsteady, Claire asked, "Did Jack tell you about Hemsley?"

"Hemsley? No."

We began, perfunctorily at first, but then in increasing detail, to unwind the story of the Dusky Gents and their dealings. Sir Hastings sat on the corner of the table, the better to listen and as he listened, an enlarged personality manifested itself. His questions were shrewd, his memory not only of the house, but of all that we told him, was acute. We could almost hear his mind working.

"That won't do," he said from time to time. "Won't do at all! Have to see what we can do! Good Lord! Not much I can teach you fellows, obviously, but perhaps it's just as well I came home when I did." Rising on his toes, he planted an unselfconscious kiss on Claire's cheek, shook me warmly by the hand and set off up the street. The last we heard of him as he rounded the corner was a rumbling and no more selfconscious belch.

When we got into the office next day I could only suppose that the much enduring Odysseus had been up all night because he seemed to know exactly what we had been doing, seemed to have read every file, seemed to have run an eye over every drawing and greeted us all with a stream of congratulations and admonition and adorned all that he had to say with a number of pointed anecdotes. At the end of this session, Heather was undaunted, Byam and I felt as though we'd been through the wringer and even Ron looked a little pale. Sir Hastings was undimmed. Brushing a few biscuit crumbs from his waistcoat, grounding his coffee cup and throwing the butt of a cigar at but not into the fireplace, he rose to his feet, "Well, I'd better get up to London," he said.

"London?" said Byam and I in chorus.

"Don't you think you'd better settle for a day or two?" said Ron.

"You must be daft!" said Heather.

"No, no," said Sir Hastings, "Got to sort this Hemsley business out. Might as well get on with it. Carpe diem, don't you know. Heather – pack me a bag, ring the club and book me a room. Ring Bertie and tell him I'll come and see him between five and six this evening. And if you can get hold of George Hardcastle, tell him to come and have lunch with me tomorrow – the club, about one o'clock."

"What on earth is he up to?" I asked Ron when the tumult of Sir Hastings' departure had subsided.

"Well, Bertie – that's Bertie Molyneux – is Permanent Secretary at the Ministry ... and Hardcastle? Well he never minds having a go in his papers at Carter who was the Minister when Hemsley Castle was sold! Keep an eye on the Sundays! Well, we shall see what we shall see, but, he's a good old ferret when he gets going, is Sir Hastings! Wouldn't be a bit surprised if there were a few bunny rabbits wondering what bit them, and Ali Baba might be one of them!"

Characteristically, Sir Hastings was not away for the half day which he had promised and we didn't see him for three days. When at last he came back, chortling with triumph, and ebullient with achievement, "I've put the cat among the pigeons!" he said with satisfaction. "There's no doubt about it, these fellows are in breach of the contract they signed when they purchased the place. Can't imagine why it wasn't spotted before. Should have been picked up! Some maladministration there. Get enough publicity rolling and we'll astonish them yet!"

Indeed, it became clear that Sir Hastings had managed to lay a considerable powder trail which in due course gave rise to a continuous series of minor explosions. Articles here and there in the serious press gave way even to headlines in the tabloids – 'Knight storms Fawlty Castle!' was my favourite. But there were others – 'Crusader Conservationist Slams Sons of Saladin'. Thus the popular press, but a long article in a more serious paper quoting freely from Sir Hastings appeared under the headline – 'The Second Battle Of Hastings'

By goodness knows what means, but by now Sir Hastings had ceased to surprise us, it was even arranged that Byam, to his unspeakable joy, appeared for a little under half a minute on a semi-serious chat show called Eastern Angles. ('Which on earth am I going to wear?' said Byam distractedly as he set off for this momentous occasion, standing in the office, his hands draped with ties. 'The bow tie? – No, too arty. The old school tie might be best, but will it show on camera? Or what about this spotted number?')

Whether this had anything to do with Byam's brief appearance or not, I really don't know, but thereafter the process of repossession began to run. "It was my tie that did it," said Byam modestly when, six months later, the Ismailia Property Company withdrew. To tell the truth, I think, they were glad enough to go. Mr. Al-Khalil's attention span was long exhausted and I really do not think he had the faintest idea why he had bought the house in the first place.

"You never know with these blokes," said Ron, "Just a way of keeping up with the Al-Jonses, if you were to ask me!"

Chapter Thirteen

Planning Blight.

"What I need," said Byam, "is several cups of tea, a couple of scones and maybe a slice of fruit cake."

I agreed that that was what I needed too. We had spent a day in which, owing to poor strategic planning, we had had no lunch, tramping round a hundred acres of abandoned orchard, derelict industry and the débris of a disused airfield, listening to the grandiose plans of a client who was hoping – erroneously, we were convinced – that he would get Planning Consent for the erection of 400 houses on what he had, with a certain amount of bleak humour, decided to call 'Adventurer's Fen'. Quite unable to persuade him of his error, and totally convinced that we had wasted a day, we had parted with false smiles, cordial handshakes and a good deal of mutual disliking.

As Byam had said when we got back into our car, "Some you lose!"

"I'll tell you what we'll do," he continued as we drove into the suburbs of Cambridge, we'll go and call on Beattie and get a cup of tea off her. You'll do much better at Beatties," he added, "than you would at my flat."

"Beattie?"

"Yes, Beattie, my sweetie! I suppose you could say she was my landlady when I was at Cambridge. She's got a newsagent's shop, tobacconist, sweetshop, tins of baked beans, and that sort of thing. Just off the Newmarket Road. Tiny little shop but a surprisingly big site behind it and, amazingly enough, a sort of stable block at the end of her yard – three rooms and a bathroom upstairs and a large coach-house downstairs. I lived there for three years and Beattie Sullivan was, as the saying goes, a mother to us all. There was me and John Prothero and Freddie Kennedy and we managed to make ourselves very comfortable. There was a perfectly good fireplace in the coach-house and, although it got a bit nippy in mid winter, we were the envy of the college. Not the envy of Beattie however, she was desperately sorry that nice young gentlemen like us had to live in 'that ratty old place'. We were never able to persuade her otherwise although we kept putting the rent up.

"No, she was wonderful to us and I'm ashamed that I've been back in Cambridge for a year already and this is the first time I've thought of coming to see her."

We drifted on past the Fen Ditton turning, past St. Bartholomew's Chapel and into the squalid straggle of the Newmarket Road where Byam suddenly turned right down a little street where a dusty notice proclaimed 'Wrestlers' Court'. Closing the end of this cul de sac was a small double fronted shop over which a fascia announced 'Tobacconist L. SULLIVAN Newsagent'. To the left a shabby pair of green painted yard gates led, I guessed, to Byam's former stable block.

A large number of children were playing in the street and the women gossiping at their front doors turned to eye us curiously. It was a friendly and in many ways an old fashioned scene where Beattie Sullivan's shop formed an agreeable curtain at the end of the cul de sac and, heralded by a jangling bell on a spring, we made our way into the dark interior.

As Byam had said, there were ranks of sweet jars, tins of baked beans, a few children's clothes, some locally knitted things on sale in aid of the restoration of the local Gospel Hall, a sack or two of chicken food and a sack labelled 'rabbit pellets'. The only item seeming to have any connection with the twentieth century was a large chest freezeer from which three little black children were seriously selecting ice creams. Their choice made, their leader called, "Bye, Mrs. Sullivan. That's a Zoom, a Cariocachoc and two Sneakers. Money on the counter,' and they clattered out of the shop.

"Goodbye dear," came a placid voice and for the first time in the gloom I noticed a neat snow-white head behind the counter.

"Beattie," said Byam, "How are you?" and Mrs. Sullivan emerged into the dim light in the front of the shop, hardly taller standing than she had been sitting on a chair.

"Who...?" She pushed her reading glasses onto her forehead and peered up at Byam. "Good Heavens! Well! It's never..? Mr. Alexander! And who's this? Is it Mr. Kennedy? No, Mr. Prothero is it...?"

"No, this is my friend Jack Simpson and, Beattie, do you still keep those little panatellas? You do? Good, I'll have a packet and – I say – Beattie – a cup of tea?"

"Well, Mr. Alexander! I'll say! You don't change! Yes, I've got some. Here you are. And a cup of tea of course! Well, well, it must be five years! And yet it seems like yesterday. Come in. Come round the counter into the back room. This is a surprise! It was only last week Mrs. Morgan was in – you remember Mrs. Morgan? She was saying what had ever happened to you all?"

We followed her into the back room and the sweetshop smell with its undertone of rabbit food and paraffin was replaced by a smell of baking.

"You must have known I'd just got a tray of scones to take out," and to me – "Reach that tin off the shelf would you Mr. Simpson? There's a bit of cake left. I'll just stir the fire. Sit down, you must be frozen this horrid day. Oh, it is good to see you! And what are you doing now?.. Well fancy!.. Not married yet then? .. Whatever happened to Hermione and that Fiona? And what was that other one... Lucy was it?"

And then to me, "Oh, we had some rare old times those years when Mr. Alexander was here... Always something happening! All those parties! You should have seen the yard in those days. I'll never forget Mr. Prothero and those Chinese lanterns! Poor Mr. Prothero! We followed his court case you know. I had a Christmas card from him last year from Marbella I think. Tax haven would that be?"

Did I catch a twinkle in the innocent blue eye?

"You really brightened up this poor old place though," she went on.

"It wasn't a poor little old place at all," protested Byam, "You never knew how lucky we thought we were! Everybody envied us you know. They used to call it the Palace."

"The Palace! So they did! I'd forgotten that! Not much of a palace now though."

Byam and I demolished a plate of Beattie's scones and most of a large cake. The room was warm. I drank my tea gratefully and listened contentedly as they chatted on.

"So who's living in the Palace now?" Byam was asking.

"Oh, nobody. Mr. Prothero's brother and those other two had it after you, then there was Mr. McDonald and two friends of his but – no – there's been nobody in the Palace for two or three years now. My nephew Brian, well he's my husband's great-nephew really, Mr. Sullivan's sister's grandson... do you remember Maude? That will be her daughter's boy. He's – a surveyor would it be? He found out that I had been breaking the law all those years – should never have had lodgers – and if it hadn't been for him I might have got into trouble with the University Lodgings Bureau. Not up to standard, he said. Outside toilet and, what was the other thing he said?.. no alternative means of escape, that was it."

The day had been cold, the room was warm, Beattie's scones were comforting and the flow of reminiscent chat between her and Byam infinitely soporific. I began to drouse by the fire, to idle the social motor and let the conversation flow with the minimum attention from me. After a while, subconsciously aware perhaps of a sharpening of Byam's attention, I returned to full wakefulness.

Beattie was speaking, "Well, it's been a long time and I shall be sorry to go, but we all have to move with the times, I suppose. Brian's been ever so helpful. He got me this rate reduction and that was a help, I must say. Of course, with this Closing Order, I thought I wouldn't get anything for the old place but Brian said, 'Leave it to me,' and he's got me an offer. It's not much but every little helps I suppose and he's found me this little place over at Trumpington. At my age it's something I just have to accept. It's only one room but you're allowed to bring your own furniture with you..."

Puzzlement lay behind the bright smile with which she favoured me as she said, "You're half asleep, Mr. Simpson! Let me pour you another cup of tea."

"Closing Order?" said Byam. "Did you have a repairs notice?"

"Oh, I don't know. I don't remember one... I leave all that to Brian. Like I say, he's been ever so good."

I opened my mouth but, silenced by a look from Byam, I closed it and, after promises to come again and another short flurry of reminiscence, we took our departure.

As we drove away down Wrestlers' Court we saw the three ice cream purchasers being shepherded in through a narrow front door.

"Good Heavens! It's Mrs. Morgan! Very old mate of mine. She used to mind the shop for Beattie. Hello Mrs. Morgan! I saw the children in Beattie's just now but I would never have recognised them... let me think now... Elliott and Angeline and – oh dear – I'm afraid I've forgotten your name, but then, you were only that long when I last saw you!"

"Byam! It's Byam Alexander! Well it's a treat to see you again! The kids won't know you behind that moustache! And you never did hear Damien's name because we hadn't christened him before you left.

"Have you been to see Beattie? Isn't it a shame! We'd have bought that little shop off her. Now it's got to be closed and the old Court won't be the same without Beattie and that's a shame because there's lots of new people. They'd sooner just pop down the Court than go all the way in to the supermarket in town across those main roads. We were going to buy it last year – we'd agreed a price with Beattie. We were going to stock it up fully and do videos as well – the nearest outlet's a good mile away. It would have made a good little business... but..." her voice trailed away and she shrugged her shoulders crossly.

"Let me guess – Brian put his oar in?" suggested Byam.

"Yes! He was furious when he heard. Came round here and warned us off. He wasn't very pleasant about it either! Told us not to mess about with his arrangements – *his*! Gave us all kinds of stuff about Closing Orders and Compulsory Demolition. Quoted Council reference numbers at us. Well, we just gave up the idea. Not much you can do really... Beattie listens to him. He's her only living relation now since her brother died so I suppose you can't blame her."

The children, growing restive with all this adult conversation, took their leave, announcing that they were just going up the meadow and was that all right?

"And what about Wrestlers Meadow?" asked Byam. "If Beattie's house gets flattened it will be opened up to the main road. There'll be people parking on it before you can say knife..." he went on speculatively.

"It looks as though we'll have seen the last of Wrestlers Meadow. They said it was a dangerous and dirty old place but the children have always played there. Bram and I did our courting there like most people from round here! It does seem a shame! And who wants *another* Business Park? Cambridge is full of them! You can't move for Business Parks, Science Parks and Enterprise Zones! There's nowhere left for just *people*! Still, I musn't go on about it. Tell me how you are getting on."

The conversation flowed on in a manner now familiar to me with enquiries about the whereabouts and recent fortunes of Messrs. Prothero and Kennedy and the unforgotten heroes from the heyday of the Palace.

"Are you thinking what I'm thinking?" asked Byam as we drove away.

"That bloody Brian!"

"Yes, that bloody Brian, you're not kidding! What about that! Dirty work at the crossroads, if you ask me. Closing Order indeed! Might be one for the U.S. Marines do you think? Just let's drive round the back. Now let me see... Wrestlers Meadow? I think we take a right and then a right... "

We proceeded accordingly and found ourselves in a rough, tussocky field of about two acres.

"There's a short cut down here to Chesterton and the river," said Byam. "Back access off the main road, I suppose... Business Park... hmm. What's young Brian's angle I wonder and who's this purchaser he's found?"

"Ransom strip do you think?" I asked.

"Yes, I'm sure that's it. Take Beattie's shop out and there's your access. How about that then? There's no other way I can see that they could get a sufficiently wide access for an enterprise of that size. I bet that's what it's all about."

And as we drove on, "Yes, I bet that's what it's all about! This is your technique – you get a Closing Order on Beattie's shop, its value goes down to zero, some sharp mate of Brian's buys it in at the bottom of the market, doing Auntie Beattie a favour you see and sells it on to the Developers for half a million quid. The Developers get their access, Brian and his mate share out the loot..."

"And Beattie moves into an Old Person's Dwelling in Trumpington?" I said.

"Well, you must admit that's what it sounds like."

A few days later, I found Byam with a heap of ragged drawings and a battered photograph album.

"What's all this?" I asked.

"Well, test your powers of observation. See if you can recognise the place."

I looked at the floor plans, seemingly of a small house. I looked at the elevations. No, not a small house, a small stable building. Outside staircase, double doors, pump fixed to the wall.

"Come on!" said Byam. "Come on, wake up!"

"No idea."

"It's Wrestlers Court. It's Beattie's stable building. The Palace."

"Good Heavens! Where did you get these from?"

"I'd quite forgotten about it but when I was at Cambridge there was a problem with the University Lodgings Bureau. I did a little drawing to prove that the Palace was equipped with every mod.con. In the end, and for some reason, the rules changed and I never had to use it. Couldn't imagine I'd ever kept the drawing until I sorted through some old stuff last night and there it was!"

"What are you planning?"

"Well, look here, we've got the excellent Mrs. Morgan raring to buy the place. Here's the stable block, terribly delapidated but fundamentally nothing wrong with it, those are thirteen and a half inch walls, you know. It faces due south and this is what we do. We get the Closing Order lifted and apply for planning permission to do the conversion. Easy – we don't even need to tell Beattie – just sign the forms as her agent. With permission granted she can then sell the shop to Mrs. Morgan and use the purchase money to convert the stable block. The Business Park doesn't get its back entrance. Wrestlers Court retains its shop and the Meadow remains the squalid old piece it is at the moment for the children to play in and for the lads and lasses of the village a place to go for a cosy snuggle of a summer evening. Beattie doesn't have to go and live in Trumpington, we could tart the courtyard up quite a lot (I shall call it 'walled garden' on the drawings) and- above all – we say nothing of what we're doing to Master Brian until the very last minute and when he and his mate come running round with their cheque for twopence halfpenny, they find their cosy little deal has gone up the creek."

"Hold on! You're forgetting two things."

"Oh, what have you in mind?"

"I have in mind the thought that perhaps Beattie might like to benefit from the odd half million it seems her property might be worth! We could just blow the gaff on young Brian and help her negotiate the sale. She could retire to the south of France if she wanted to or even buy a small house on the Hills Road for that kind of money. And secondly, she might not want to upset her nephew if he's all she's got."

"Knowing Beattie, I'm sure she would want to end her days where she was born and brought up if she can only be given the chance and

I know she doesn't hold with Business Parks!"

"You may be right, but all the same," I said feeling I was sounding rather too holy, "she ought to be given all the facts and allowed to make up her own mind. All her life I bet men have been making decisions for her, right down to this pillock of a nephew. And now you're doing the same thing – knowing what's best for Beattie!"

He had the grace to look embarrassed and mumbled that perhaps I was right and, leave it to him, he would get it sorted out by the time I got back from my holiday.

I rather lost touch with Byam and with Beattie's affairs at this point because Claire and I took an often postponed and much needed fortnight's holiday returning late one Friday night to an icy house. For all its charm, number 14 the Pottergate was the least heat-retentive structure I have ever experienced.

I lit the fire, carried in the goodies from Normandy, set tins of paté, Livarot cheese and bottles of this and that out on the kitchen table and Claire disappeared upstairs to wash her hair. She is not capable of coming back from anywhere (or for the matter of that going anywhere) without separating the journey from real life by this ritual and was accordingly sitting on the floor in front of the fire drying her hair when, above the roar of the hair-dryer, I heard a thunderous knock on the front door which I opened to reveal Byam.

"Oh, man!" he said without preamble. "Wow! Have I ever got some news for you!" Then, "Oh, hello, Claire! What ho! The only blonde golliwog at present in captivity, I see." He went on, "What a day! What a triumph! Wow! Just wait till I tell you guys – your uncle Byam is a genius!"

"Quick!" I said to Claire, "Fetch the sal volatile! Loosen his stays! Dash some water in his face! I've seen these cases before and it's not a very pretty sight! Expect increasing hysteria to lead to catatonia and possibly even death!"

"Oh, bugger the sal volatile!" said Byam, "Pull a few corks out! I really have got something to tell you. Now, just cast the little old mind back to little old Beattie and the Bandit Brian."

While he was talking I found a bottle of duty free vodka, a few bottles of tonic, slightly flat, but freshened with a good deal of ice and Byam resumed, "Well, you may remember that I was in the throes of a drawing for the conversion of the palace into a retirement home for our Beattie? To say nothing of a schedule to get this closing order lifted. It was a damned good drawing, although I say it myself. Little bits of paving here and there, a small tree or two, plenty of cast shadow – you know – the usual sort of thing. I was so pleased with it, I shoved it in for planning."

He took a gulp of vodka so formidable that his eyes began to water and it was some time before he could resume. "Shoved it in for planning – not from the office – under my own name from Cambridge. So what happened? I got back to the flat one night and Johnny said to me ...."

"Johnny?"

"Johnny Bennet, the man I share a flat with, and he said to me, 'A man called Landers has rung you about six times. He seemed very steamed up. He wants you to ring him back on this number.' Landers? thought I. Who's Landers? But being a cooperative sort of bloke I duly rang him back and who do you think Landers turned out to be? None other than Beatties's magically seductive nephew! Bloody Brian! -

'Ah, Mr. Alexander! Got you at last! You're a very elusive young man, you know.'" Byam's voice took on a fruity and gin-fogged tone with an underlying rasp of menace. "That's rather good," he said, appraising his own imitation and he went on, "'I think you've been rather a naughty boy! Put in an application on Wrestler's Court did you? Not quite playing the game, was it? Filling my poor aunt's head full of nonsense? We don't do that sort of thing, Mr. er... Alexander. I expect, as you well know, my firm are acting for Mrs. Sullivan and you're acting without instructions. I've got a very nice little deal stitched together with Mrs. Sullivan and I don't want you muddying the water. So far this is just friendly advice – keep off the grass – get it? That's all. You withdraw that application and we'll say no more about it, OK? I said OK?'"

"How old's this Brian?" I asked.

"Well, from the tone, I'd guess in his mid fifties."

"Mid fifties? I thought we were dealing with a beardless lad."

"Yes, I thought we were dealing with a beardless lad too, but there's no reason why we should be – Beattie after all is in her eighties, so Brian is likely to be in his fifties. Anyway, he went on – 'Now I'm not blaming you, Mr., er, beyond a point. We all had our way to make in the world once upon a time. You're a young man, got to get the work where you can, but you start conning some poor old age pensioner into giving you a job and nobody's going to like you. I'm not going to like you, but you just do what I tell you, laddie, and you may not be the loser. I haven't heard the name before. Just started out in practice have you? Well I can remember what it was like and I might be able to do you a bit of good. Done any development work have you?' And a lot more in the same vein. I listened to this garbage, planning a blistering reply, but eventually I thought 'I'll kill him! Later!' so I listened with what I'm sure he took to be respectful attention." He paused, "I say, could we have something to eat? I'm starving! I've got a lot more to tell you."

We adjourned to the kitchen and sorted through the loot from

France, returning to the fire with bottles and butter and tins of paté, a cheese or two, a droopy baguette and a squashed almond tart. Byam resumed,

"As I say, I decided to kill him. So what did I do? Next time I was in the office, and speaking as Sir Hastings Munro – well, that's not quite true, I actually said I was Mr. Simpson (I knew you wouldn't mind and, after all, I could hardly appear in the guise of Alexander, the newly qualified and upwardly mobile tiny Cambridge architect) – so, in the character of Simpson speaking for Sir Hastings I rang Brian and said I understood that his firm were handling the matter of Wrestlers Meadow and that we had clients who would be more than interested in acquiring the site and who would be prepared to make a fair offer for it and that we understood that he was in the process of negotiating the question of access. My dear! He nearly burst a blood vessel! – How had I heard? Never heard such nonsense in all his life! What did I say my name was? I said vaguely that I had heard on the Cambridge grapevine – these sort of rumours get around – you know how it is! Would it be possible for me to make a direct approach to the client and so on. Scared him shitless! The last thing in the world he wants is somebody sniffing round the site who might conceivably make Beattie a fair offer for the store. Thought that would force his hand and encourage him to make his move...

"So far, so good! Then I thought that maybe the time had come to go public with Beattie and tell her what I was up to and tactfully try to explain that nephew Brian wasn't exactly the Holy Apostle Paul so, one evening, I popped round to see her – usual scene – shop swarming with kids, Beattie busy selling baked beans and shoe laces... telephone begins to ring...'Oh, could you answer that for me?' says Beattie from the deep freeze." Byam began to laugh at the memory of his cleverness or his luck...

"'Byam? Is that you? Gerry's being trying to get you all day! Hold on while I put you through.' Rather a mystery as I think you'll agree. Not Heather's normal style and, anyway, who the Hell's Gerry? All was to be revealed. A husky voice, 'Brian? Brian? I say, have you said anything?'

"'Said anything?' I said rather stupidly.

"'Oh, come on Brian! Wake up! Have you said anything to the old lady?'

"All was plain! Gerry must be the loathsome Brian's partner and he hadn't asked for 'Byam' at all! They thought I was Brian! OK – I was quite prepared to be Brian! So, assuming my Brian voice, which I can tell you is pretty good, the conversation went like this -

"'I say, have you said anything to the old lady?'

"Self – 'Said anything to the old lady? What about?'

"Gerry – 'Said anything about the option?'

"No, s'aright, I haven't said anything yet.

"Gerry – 'Well, listen, Brian, boy – abort! Back off!'

"I thought it would be sensible to ask – 'Why, when we've got so far?'

"'Because Fairdeal have pulled out of Wrestlers Meadow! We've just heard from our contact. It's not worth a sausage! The buggers have changed their minds and decided to go somewhere else!'

"Such was his excitement that I thought I could risk a slightly longer speech – 'I'm reading you,' I said. 'What made them do that?'

There was no doubt about it – Byam had got his audience. Claire and I stopped eating. We even stopped drinking.

"So go on," I said breathlessly, "What happened next?"

"Well not much more from Master Gerry, because at that moment a very large motor car drew up outside and the crowd in the shop was augmented by a particularly nasty looking piece of work whom I had no problem at all in identifying as Brian. He set the children on one side, put his hands on the counter, produced an envelope from his pocket and, his eye beaming with insincerity, his face disfigured by a smile of non charm, he said to Beattie, 'I've brought the papers, Auntie. Here's the cheque. All you have to do is sign – here.'

"'Sign? Sign what?'

"Well I guessed and it was subsequently confirmed that he had brought round a six month option in favour of his company on the shop and a cheque for ten thousand pounds. Can you believe it? I'd so put the wind up him with the idea of another punter that he and the unspeakable Gerry had decided to nail Beattie down with an option while they completed their deal with Fairdeal. What Gerry was anxious to convey to Brian was that Fairdeal had dropped out and he was not to sell the option and, above all, he was not to part with ten thousand pounds."

"Option?"

"Yes, an option to purchase the shop within six months. The idea was, that with a closing order on the shop, it was worth very little indeed. Brian and Gerry could pick it up at any time within the forthcoming six months which would give them time to stitch their deal together with the supermarket chain and sell it on for a few hundred thousand quid. So intent was Brian on getting his deal that he didn't even notice me, shrunk as I was into a narrow recess at the back of the shop and sitting on a bag of rabbit pellets. But now, we've frustrated his knavish tricks and he's also given Beattie a present of ten thousand pounds for an option to purchase the shop which, without the spin off from Fairdeal he won't be able to afford because, by that time, the closing order will have been lifted and planning consent will have been granted for the conversion of the palace into a damn nice little cottage for Beattie while the excellent Mrs. Morgan zeroes in on the shop and buys it for a fair price which she is only too anxious to do."

My head was beginning to spin under this information overload but I smiled encouragingly and let Byam rave on.

"How did Beattie take it, finding out that her nephew was a rogue?" asked Claire. "How on earth did you break it to her?"

"Do you know, I think she had her suspicions from the outset... I certainly didn't need to spell it out for her. And, come to think of it... she didn't suggest giving him his cheque back which I was afraid she might!"

"Byam, you're wonderful!" said Claire, her eyes shining, I was sorry to see, with hero worship.

Byam, smirking with quiet satisfaction, bowed to his audience and began to make for the door. Hand on the knob, he paused and said as though by afterthought, "Oh, by the way, do you remember Mr. Goodman? Adventurer's Fen in Cambridge? That awful piece of industrial deadland we looked at with him? Well, he's given us instructions to draw up a scheme for him. Seems a supermarket chain called Fairdeal have decided it's just where they want to place their Cambridge branch. Plenty of space and no access problems..."

"Byam, you're wonderful," I said, my eyes shining with hero worship.

Chapter Fourteen.

The Cricket Match.

Christmas that year was on a Wednesday so, one way and another, when we returned from holiday we were confronted by about ten days' accumulated mail. Sir Hastings had been to the States for Christmas and was not expected back for another week and Heather had been to stay with her sister in Newcastle so, when I finally persuaded the front door to open through the drift of letters banked in the hall, I entered a bleak and empty house. Such was the build up of envelopes round my feet I was constrained to find a basket to carry them up to the office where I was joined by Ron and where we settled down in a companionable silence punctuated at intervals by comment and conjecture to sort the accumulation into its respective piles.

Thus, Ron –

"Here's a certificate application from Johnson's! I thought that job was finished... We're going to have to do something about that account from Marstock. This is the second application... Oh, hallo, planning consent for phase 2 at Aldringham and about time too... One here addressed to the Executive de Cadre, Personnel Liaison... Who's that? Another new appointment?"

"No, Ron, that's Eurospeak for pass this on to someone important in the firm. Put it on Heather's pile. She'll know what to do with it."

"What's this? Looks like the 'Prince of Wales'. It is the 'Prince of Wales'!" He held up a Christmas card the size of a drawing board with the legend 'Best wishes for a prosperous New Year from Constable Construction.'

I forced this into the waste paper basket but put a large robin on a small log 'With best wishes to all at Spring House from Tom and Iris' on the mantelpiece, displacing to make room for it a spring-loaded card from a firm of sanitary fitting manufacturers called Situpon from which there leapt when you opened it a horribly graphic representation of their revolutionary pop-up flushing system.

And so we worked our way forward. The individual piles grew steadily, the basket began to overflow with junk mail – seasonal or otherwise. After a while Ron's flow of cheerful chatter was interrupted by an extraordinary exclamation of vivid disgust. "Struth!" he said. "What the Hell? What bastard wrote this? Jesus!"

"What's the problem Ron?"

"It's a letter to Sir H. I don't know! Sort of thing makes you want to give up or throw up or both!" He fell silent for a moment looking at the letter in his hand and began to speak again, "It's from the churchwarden at Windlesham. Sir H. has been working there for fifteen years. It's the most perfectly restored church in the county. He's won a couple of craftsmanship awards, never charged them the full fee!"

I had never heard Ron speak with such bitterness. "Churches!" he said, "Nine out of ten – no, more than that – ninety nine out of a hundred are as good as gold. The rectors? Some good and some bad. Some answer your letters but quite a lot don't. Well-meaning if you see what I mean but they're busy. Leave a lot to us and that's OK. We work it out together. You get bad jobs and you get good jobs. Sometimes you make a bob or two but more often you don't. And the Parochial Church Council secretaries and the churchwardens – they're just the same. Mostly take the job on because there's nobody else, but, at the end of the day it's the job that counts and you can stand back and say 'Well that turned out all right. Ought to keep the old place together for another hundred years,' and you get on and do the next one. But just occasionally... just occasionally... and I can think of perhaps three times in the last thirty years you meet a real wrong 'un. Some newcomer in the village comes down to teach us country chaps how it ought to be done, you know. Thinks he knows it all. 'Oh,' says he, 'I'll take over the fabric fund, the appeals committee or whatever it might be. But he's not interested in the job or the church – he's just interested in himself – playing the squire – probably got an unsatisfactory job – not getting on with the Missis – here's a chance to be the Great I Am but doesn't know arse from elbow. Everybody else in the parish is busy and probably only too glad to let him get on with it. Doesn't happen often but there's something about the Church – when you get a bad one, they're rotten! We've got a right one 'ere!"

I read down the middle of the letter he handed me. Various phrases sprang from the paper -

"It is apaling that a so called proffesional is able to practice and charge so much for doing so little... May I suggest that practice is the oparative word in your case!!!... Talking about your final accounts, you will have to strenuously justify same in the light that legaly a good or service must be of merchantable quality and I cannot accept that you have given us a service at all!!! ... Your sloppy approach may have been acceptable fourty years ago but now we expect something a bit more proffesional!... I wish to reiterate my statements over the telephone that in view of your proffesional incompetetence, apon cessation of this matter, I intend, on beharf of the PCC to dispense with your SO CALLED services!!!"

A flourishing and illegible signature at the end was followed by the name Ian Bentley.

"What's Sir H. going to say about this?" I said at last.

"Well, if it wasn't Windlesham, I'd say he wouldn't give a toss. If we've got some little Hitler the other side of the fence who can't read the file and who wouldn't understand if he did, he'd say 'Let it go.'

"Too proud to fight?" I asked.

"That sort of thing," said Ron. "But Windlesham's pretty special for him. Lady Munro's buried there for a start. I know they spent hours there, praying, the months before she died... and now this bugger, who's been in the village all of two minutes..." His normally placid face was distorted for a moment with revulsion.

At this moment, Byam sauntered through the door.

"Gawd! What a Christmas!" he said. "Have I ever got a hangover! You're lucky to see me at all!"

"Lucky?" I said, "Would you say lucky?" And indeed, eyes were unattractively encarnadine and set in a pale shade of yellow. "Portrait of an English gentleman in the last stages of amorous exhaustion," I said.

"'Is Lordship 'as drunk 'is bath and gone back to bed again," said Ron. "Better if you had!"

Byam slumped in a chair beside us and idly picked up the letter from the parish of Windlesham. "What's this shower?" he said, waking to attention. "Who's this oaf? What the Hell?"

We explained. "Did the old feller make a balls of it?" asked Byam.

"Not likely!" said Ron who had seen the job. "But you know what Sir H. is like. Not one to suffer fools gladly or at all. He was probably a bit sharp with this bloke. He can be sometimes. Must have told him a thing or two that didn't quite suit his dignity.

Byam read the letter again. "This is libellous, you know," he said seriously. "If this yobbo repeats this in public at all, we could screw him for libel."

"He won't do that if I know the type," I said. "Letter's full of half understood snippets of legalese. No, I should think he's calculated fairly carefully just how far he can go and he probably knows Sir Hastings would never take a step in the matter."

"He may not take a step in the matter, but I can," said Byam. "I'll kill him! The curse of the Alexanders shall descend on him. I won't let him go! You'll see! He'll trip on the chancel steps, fall and fracture both kneecaps, upset the whole of the offertory down through a floor grating. On Easter Sunday. Talking of offertory – what's the parson doing in all this?"

"Useless, quite useless!" said Ron. "This bloke's obviously got him by the short and curlies. Happens sometimes."

Byam wrote a blistering rebuke, warned that if any of the allegations were repeated an action for libel would follow and there the matter rested until Sir Hastings returned but – as Ron had predicted – he refused to take any step in the matter.

"Only flatters chaps like that if you take any notice of them," he said peaceably. "You know how it is -

'.................... man, proud man,
Dressed in a little brief authority,
Most ignorant of what he is most assured,
His glassy essence like an angry ape,
Performs such fantastic tricks before high Heaven,
As make the angels weep.'"

"That's all very well," said Byam, "and I quite agree, but I don't think you should let this go!"

"Come, come, me dear boy! Have a little dignity! Chaps don't have to get down and roll in the mud with chaps like that, you know. He knows he's talking balls. We know he's talking balls. Nothing we say or do would persuade him to admit it. Feel sorry for the feller really."

"Buggered if I do!" said Byam venomously.

"Now Smithson!" said Sir Hastings imperturbably, "Remember what the great Jowett said – 'Never complain, never explain, never apologise.' I think the point of that was that fellers of whom it is necessary to complain or who need an explanation or an apology aren't worth having."

"Aren't you even going to answer?" asked Byam desperately.

"Answer? My dear fellow! Good Heavens, no! Like the Duke of Wellington, if I answered every footling letter I received, I'd have no time to get on with the active business of campaigning! Haw, haw, haw! No, No, let's have a look at the amended drawings on those cloakrooms at what's the name of the place.

"I'll tell you a funny thing – when I was young, I was working on the scheme for a hospital. Boring? Deadly boring! There was a detached block at the back called the Sanitary Annexe and, do you know? I was just lettering up the drawing when I went out to lunch. Came back, had fifty copies made, quite forgot I hadn't finished the drawing and blow me! – copies went to all members of the committee. This little block was labelled 'Sanitary Anne'. Haw, haw! Matron's name was – well you fellers can guess what the Matron's name was! Thought I'd done it on purpose! Nearly got the sack! Haw, haw! And in a similar sort of way, don't you know, a friend of mine did a measured drawing of Saint. Mary Aldermary. He said to me,

'I've never been able to do a good capital S. I wish you'd put the capital S on here for me.'

"'No trouble, me boy,' I said. What did I do – completely forgot! Drawing went in for this competition titled 'aint Mary the Virgin'! Shows you can't be too careful! All the same – it's a shame about Windlesham... Done some good work there in me time."

We weren't fooled by all this carry-on. We saw that Sir Hastings minded quite a lot and Byam was the more resolved to wreak his revenge on the evil Mr. Bentley.

All the more resolved when, the following month, we were informed that the PCC of Windlesham were indeed to dispense with Sir Hastings' professional services and would, henceforth, be engaging the services of an up and coming architect whose only special qualification for the job appeared to be that he was the cousin of churchwarden Bentley. And that was what it was all about of course, we realised – the bloody minded attitude had been quite deliberately adopted to force Sir Hastings to resign and when he didn't they had forced him out anyway. Our contempt for the man deepened.

We had, however, quite a long time to wait before we could wreak the revenge we had sworn. It wasn't, in fact, until the following summer and it came about in an unusual way.

We had been pressed for some time to visit Colonel Lindsay Ross at Little Hampden and collect some bedding plants that he had got ready for us. Accordingly, in late June, Claire and I with Byam made our way to Oak Farm where we were received, as of old, and with open arms by Iris.

"Tom will be back in a minute – back in time for tea, anyway. He's down on the meadow, rolling the cricket pitch. Important match on Sunday. Against Windlesham."

At that moment Tom came perspiring into the kitchen, burnished by the sun to the colour of a not quite ripe Victoria plum. "Ah," he said, "there you are! Sorry I wasn't here to greet you. Got a needle match on Sunday. Silly sort of business really but there's a fellow in the next village – Windlesham you know – don't like him much – pretentious sort of chap – presented a cup to be played for between the two villages. Of course, Windlesham is much bigger than we are. I suppose he thought he'd walk all over us but one of the rules was that if either side won the cup three years running then they could keep it. Win it outright you know. Well we didn't think much of this because I don't think that until this nonsense started we'd ever beaten Windlesham in our lives," the colonel paused and imbibed the best part of a cup of tea. "Then old John Soper moved his little haulage business onto the old airfield (a lot of people opposed it but I always thought it was a good idea; it employs six or seven local chaps and that's what we need around here) and it turned out he'd got two sons – Rory and Kevin – good lads. They run the business with him. But the point is – Kevin turned out to be a fast bowler and Rory turned out to be what we'd always been looking for which is a wonderful opening bat. Just what we needed! Course – Master Bentley hadn't reckoned on that when he presented the 'Bentley Cup'. 'Bentley Cup' indeed!

"So there was Kevin knocking them down like ninepins and young Rory made 83 not out last year. The first year we won by four wickets and last year we won by six wickets." The Colonel smiled with reminiscent triumph. Then his face grew serious.

"Not going to happen this year though! In fact, I don't know what we're going to do! I was half inclined to cancel."

"Why? What's happened?" I asked.

"Well old John Soper, he's just a rough old Suffolk chap, and what does he do? Gets himself into trouble with the VAT inspector. No proper returns, no proper records, never bothered to register, tremendous amount of his business is probably done in cash or kind... they caught up with him. Kevin and Rory never had a great deal to do with that side of the business. Now old Soper's had a stroke! These poor lads have got to appear before an enquiry on Monday. They didn't know anything about it until yesterday. The old man hadn't said anything to them. Goodness knows what he thought would happen! Yesterday young Kevin came round to see me. Terrible distress poor chap! Got to spend the weekend sorting through the firm's business for the last three years. Try to get some sort of statement together, looking up their records for the period. But the long and the short of it is that neither of them can play on Sunday. That leaves us weak, very weak.

"No, it looks as if the Bentley Cup will go back to Windlesham, because," he turned to Iris and said, "I didn't tell you this, did I? Something else I discovered today – can you guess what Mr. Bentley does for a living? Works for Customs and Excise – in the VAT department. I'll bet that's what's happened! He's shopped old Soper and stitched these lads up so that they can't play on Sunday!"

"Oh, Tom," said Iris, "How can you say so! You can't believe that!"

"Wouldn't put anything past him!" said the Colonel.

"Eighty three not out," said Byam, "What a coincidence! My best was eighty three not out... for Winchester in the Eton match. We lost but ask anybody who was there and they'll all say the same, 'Alexander was seeing them that day!'"

He helped himself to a piece of cake, seemingly unaware of the charged silence that had fallen across the room.

"You know what you're doing on Sunday?" I said to him. "Turning out for Little Hampden!"

Byam laughed easily. "Out of the question," he said. "Years ago, perhaps, but, good Heavens! I haven't touched a bat for years!"

"You'll soon pick it up," said the Colonel eagerly, "Once a cricketer, always a cricketer, you know! Tell you what – come on down to the field with me. I'll bowl you a few in the net. It'll come back to you. What do you say?"

"I'd be useless," said Byam, "Useless!"

"Won't know that till you try," said the Colonel firmly.

Of course, we all yielded and trailed down to the field together.

"This Bentley," asked Byam as we walked through the gate at the end of the garden, "give me a word picture. About four foot six high? Bearded? Aggressive? Churchwarden? Am I thinking of the right man?"

"That sounds like him," replied the Colonel, "but perhaps a bit more than four foot six. Ginger beard, aggressive, yes, and certainly a churchwarden. He played for Bucks... or was it Berks... once or twice in his youth and, blast the feller, I have to say it – he can bat! Good bowler too, fast you know. He'd have sunk us if it hadn't been for Rory and Kevin!"

There aren't so many village cricket grounds about as there used to be, though in the sentimental imagination of many, these remain the essence of rural England. The cricket ground at Little Hampden was, however, as neat, as trim, as green, as tree-girt as nostalgia could possibly require. The pavilion was in corrugated iron painted the dull red of red oxide with white windows and white railings. The score board was still hung with the black and white plates of the last game played and displayed the legend 75 for 5 Last man 4.

The Colonel extracted a bat from the pavilion, brown with age and years of linseed oil and bound on more than one occasion with white tape. He secured two or three cricket balls, no longer truly spherical and of impressive age and a pair of pads that didn't quite match. I watched Byam with considerable amusement because it was quite clear to me that cricket madness had him in its grip; it was clear to me that he was going to turn out for the Colonel on Sunday and that he would have done so even without the chance to outsmart the evil Bentley.

He took his place in the net and the Colonel took a few elderly steps, bowled an innocuous ball well pitched up outside the off stump. Byam, playing off the back foot, delivered one of the crispest square cuts I have ever seen. The Colonel said nothing but his face was gleaming with excitement as he sent down his second delivery. A half volley this time, more or less on the wicket, to which Byam played elegantly forward and the ball trickled to my feet.

I picked it up. The seam slipped with familiarity between my first and second finger. I walked back. I took my usual run. The air was humid and close and as I ran up I thought, "It ought to swing a bit today." It did. I sent down a ball like an express train. It moved across the line. Byam played forward a little too late and, with a satisfactory click, his leg bail spun away and disappeared into the bushes through a hole at the back of the net.

"Good Lord!" said Byam.

"Good Heavens!" said the Colonel.

"Know what you're doing on Sunday?" said Byam.

I knew it already, had known it from the moment that I picked up the ball.

"I didn't know you could do that," said Byam.

"Course, he can!" said Claire who had strolled down with Iris. "Fastest thing since Freddy Trueman. 46 for 6 for Kingsdown Comprehensive against Croydon."

"46 for 6 will do very nicely on Sunday!" said the Colonel. "Half past two? Draw stumps at about seven? We're not very particular about that. Looks as if we'll have a nice day if the forecast is right." His face was wreathed in happy smiles. "I shan't say a word about this except to our own chaps," he said. "I'll tell Mr. Bentley we've got to play a pair of substitutes. Rory and Kevin will be relieved. They were very upset but I think we can astonish Mr. Bentley now!"

Byam and I made modest disclaimers – "Haven't played for years... don't know if we can still do it... might make the most terrible balls of it... don't expect too much... really only stopgaps ..." But the fever was upon us.

Chapter Fifteen

The Cricket Match (Part Two.)

"I shouldn't be doing this," I said to Claire on the morning of the match. "For starters, I've got nothing to wear."

"Go on with you," she snorted back at me, "You've got a white shirt haven't you? And I soaked those grey jeans of yours in bleach overnight – they've come up lovely! You can whiten your trainers and there you are! It's only a village cricket match after all. They'll all be looking as scruffy as you!"

"Byam won't be looking scruffy!"

Sunday was, as the Colonel had predicted, fine, but, although there was a gentle cross wind, it was, nevertheless, overcast and muggy. "Just the day for me!" I said to Claire with satisfaction. "I ought to be able to swing 'em a bit today!"

"That's the spirit! You get in there and swing 'em!" she said.

I'd played a good deal of club cricket and I was well accustomed to the sort of jokes that are enjoyed on these occasions, especially when the two teams have met each other a number of times before. Today, however, this form of camaraderie was conspicuously absent. The two teams kept themselves to themselves and the Little Hampden team were grimly intent. The Colonel in a panama hat, girt about his corpulence with an old Rugbeian silk scarf, was talking with a short bearded figure. The short bearded figure was bristling and gesticulating a lot and flashing an ingratiating smile.

"That looks like the Evil One to me," said Byam. "Curse of the Alexanders doesn't seem to have taken yet! Looks as fit as a fiddle! But – 'Boast not thyself! A frightful fiend doth close behind thee tread!'"

"Two frightful fiends!" I said and we joined the Colonel who made the introductions.

"Got to field a couple of stop-gaps today," said the Colonel. "I know you won't mind my calling you stop-gaps. We'd have been a couple short if these two hadn't stepped into the breach at the last minute," and he shot a look icy with meaning at the perky Mr. Bentley who rose and fell on the balls of his feet.

"Well, beggars can't be choosers, I suppose. And where did you say you were from exactly?" He looked us up and down, a little daunted perhaps by Byam's snowy whiteness but clearly reassured to note that my faded jeans which had looked so white on the line looked very grey indeed between my freshly whitened trainers and my immaculate white shirt, the latter obviously of a business rather than a sporting origin.

"I don't remember," said Byam coldly, "having said where we were from, exactly or otherwise." And turning to me, "Did you say where we were from? ... No, I didn't think you had. But we are, in fact, from Lavenham, a wool town in the west of the county. I am the personal assistant of Sir Hastings Munro of whom you have probably heard, an architect of matchless distinction, quite unspoilt by his enormous and so well deserved prestige and a man who would, as is often said, never harm a fly. Lucky break for flies, wouldn't you agree, Mr. Benchley? But there, although I have enjoyed this chat I mustn't detain you. Do I understand that you are the 'captain' of the Windlesham side?" And turning to me – "There, Mr. Brenchley is the captain of the Windlesham side, but as he himself would put it, 'Beggars can't be choosers.' But now you really must excuse me," and with a courteous nod he turned towards the pavilion.

"I say, Bentley, if you've any objection to these two filling in at the last moment...?" began the Colonel, hesitantly.

Mr. Bentley, still nonplussed and puzzled by Byam's contribution, took another long look at me. I grinned oafishly and kicked the head off a buttercup with my whitened trainer.

"No, Colonel ... that is ... er, no. Certainly not. Be glad to show your young men a thing or two, eh?"

Mr. Bentley stood for a moment, doubtful, and his discomfiture was augmented by the arrival of a Ferrari which, like a speedboat berthing amongst a squadron of fishing boats, came to a halt alongside the vans, Landrovers, bicycles and mopeds favoured by the Little Hampden supporters.

The Little Hampden supporters had been impressed by Byam's appearance and, no doubt, by the Colonel's advance publicity for us both. They were clearly much heartened by the appearance of Gentian who swept, waving and smiling, long legs twinkling under her short red skirt, up to the pavilion where she lost no time in donning a voluminous apron and joining Iris and Claire in the sandwich-buttering line-up.

The Colonel drew a silver five rupee piece from his pocket and duly lost the toss. Little Hampden took the field, the Colonel behind the stumps, Byam at cover point, myself at deep mid-on and a flaxen-haired youth called – I believe – Gubber – took an inordinately long run, dug a very large hole with his heel, rubbed the ball against his bottom and proceeded to bowl the opening over at ferocious speed, variable length and only fair accuracy.

The Colonel stood respectfully well back but the opening batsmen, after a moment or two of hesitation, were undaunted by Gubber's fierce attack. They had, after all, played him before and the first over produced two singles, a three and four leg byes.

At the end of this over, a local farmer came on at the other end. I wasn't expecting much from him because the Colonel had told me he'd only just got his arm out of plaster. Though the plaster had gone, his opening delivery was so harmless – a well pitched up full toss to leg that, after a split second of astonishment that anyone could bowl such a ball, the batsman gleefully dispatched it to the boundary and the second ball which was little better duly followed it. By this time the farmer was clearly demoralised because his third ball went wide and his fourth ball was a mirror repeat of delivery one or delivery two. The batsman, with two boundaries under his belt, advanced on this with relish, got an edge and delivered an easy catch to the Colonel behind the stumps. Eighteen for one. By the standards of deep Suffolk, a fair opening stand I suppose.

At first wicket down, one of those infuriating batsmen (infuriating that is to the fielding side) who greets every ball in the same way, that is to say a pace across the wicket, coming more or less to attention, and presenting a dead bat to everything on the wicket, and letting everything else go, came in. The score mounted steadily, though nearly all the runs were made at the other end until the other opening bat played across the opening delivery and was bowlėd all over the place.

I met the Colonel as we crossed over at the end of this over. "That's not bad," he said. "Thirty five for three, but we haven't got into their batting strength yet. This next feller can hit 'em sometimes and then we've got Bentley to contend with. I think I'll put Cocker Woods on and rest Farmer Alcock. There ought to be a little bit of movement in the wicket. Let's see."

Cocker Woods turned out to be the sort of bowler that every village cricket side should have – absolutely steady, absolutely safe, seldom off his length, seldom off the line, totally unenterprising who will, from time to time get a wicket because the batsman is bored and wishes to demonstrate that he is not fooled. And so it was in this case. Eventually the plodder abandoned his tactics for a mistaken second, played forward across the line, mistimed one of Cocker's easier deliveries and was out l.b.w.

A jaunty figure emerged from the pavilion and set off towards us. Byam and I stood together and observed his advance.

"But hark. the cry is Bentley," said Byam,
And lo, the ranks divide.
And the arsehole of Windlesham
Comes with his jaunty stride!"

We had good reason to detest the repulsive Bentley but I have to admit that he was a very fair bat and I could well see why he had played for Bucks or was it Berks?

He rattled his way through his first over from Cocker from which he amassed twelve runs and, with a single off the last ball, turned to face the perspiring Gubber whose length and direction, although he was visibly tiring, had improved considerably. I had to respect the caution with which Bentley played himself in and the precision with which he scored two off the fifth ball and three off the last ball, bringing himself to confront Cocker Woods.

And so the match proceeded for an over or two. The score mounted steadily to sixty and then to seventy; the batsmen seemed set for a week. I longed to get at them. But it was some time before the Colonel put me on. I felt sure he didn't want to belittle the local talent and, in my heart, I thought he was right.

But at last, with Ian Bentley on forty two and his companion on thirty eight, the Colonel said as we crossed over, "Next over, from the pavilion end, Jack."

I stepped out my run. I put a small white stone down on the grass as I always had. I moved Byam back into the slips and organised the outfield. A familiar drunkenness overcame me and I thundered down the pitch. My first ball was a honey. It pitched in the blockhole with all the speed and with many times the precision of a Scud missile, knocked the middle stump completely out of the ground and it nearly impaled the Colonel.

A stunned silence ensued to be broken by whoops and cheers from the pavilion led by Gentian, supported by Iris and Claire and by the entire population of Hampden.

"They don't like this chap much," said the Colonel, nodding towards the incoming batsman. "Quite right! Shocking fellow! On the District Council, you know. On the planning committee. Bit partial perhaps in some of his judgements, if you take my meaning. See what you can do with him!"

I couldn't do much, as it happened, and he scored two off my last ball. Ian Bentley continued to bash away at the other end and could have run an easy single off the last ball but refused the run which left me once more to confront the District Councillor who prodded the ball away successfully through five balls but, with the last, which was swinging away, he played forward too soon and gave Byam an easy catch at third slip. But, try as I might, I couldn't bring Ian Bentley into my sights. He remained discreetly at the other end. He was standing confidently out of his ground and the runs continued to come.

At last though, and from the last ball of an over, he drove confidently into the deep; there should have been two runs there but Farmer Alcock gathered the ball and returned it with such precision to the Colonel that they had to be content with a single.

"Now for it!" I thought.

As I started my run, I noticed two things – firstly that with a perky and condescending smile, Bentley was standing well out of his ground and secondly that silently the Colonel had closed up behind the stumps. I charged into action, breathing smoke, and without varying my approach, delivered the slowest ball of the match. Bentley went onto the back foot, changed his mind, came forward, missed the ball by a mile, was neatly scooped up by the Colonel a foot or more outside the crease and was stumped.

"It's an old trick," said the Colonel modestly to our congratulations. "Thought you'd get the message!"

Thereafter we went through the tail briskly enough. Windlesham were all out for 186. My figures were 5 for 45.

"Winning score?" I asked the Colonel as we settled in front of the enormous tea.

"Don't know. Very much depends on young Byam. But if everybody played their best we'd rattle them off in no time. Though we've got some good fellows, they're terribly erratic. Easily rattled, you know. If everything's going well, they go well, but if things get a bit dodgy ..."

As before, the teams kept themselves to themselves. The tension was considerable and the conversation muted. Muted that is except for Ian Bentley who addressed himself with breezy confidence to one and all.

Leaving Iris behind the teapot, Byam and I took our plates and joined Claire and Gentian on the grass.

"I don't really understand cricket but I liked the bit where you knocked that peg out!"

"Stump, dear, stump," said Byam absently. I could see that cricket madness had him in its grip.

The Colonel put himself in to open. "I don't make many runs these days," he said, "but I can sit on the splice. If I can stay there it might steady the young ones down a bit. Anchor man, don't you know!"

Iris came to join us. "I do hope he'll be all right," she said. And to me, "I don't know what we'd be chasing now if it weren't for you! Where are you batting?"

"Number eleven," I said firmly. "My highest score so far is eighteen and that was twenty years ago."

The Colonel and his partner, a huge man known to one and all as Bone (though this was his name or had any reference to his skull I never found out) proceeded demurely to the wicket. The Colonel took guard. Ian Bentley retreated to the boundary and came pounding in, his unlovely features twisted in a scowl, his eyes crossed with determination. The Colonel let everything off the wicket pass him, patted everything on the wicket demurely back down the pitch and the first over was a maiden.

Bone at the other end, shared none of the Colonel's inhibitions and laid about him like Captain Bligh. Every country cricket side seems to have a Bone. Everything that comes their way they either miss or smite with all their strength. They can – they often do – make a duck, but they can, and Bone did, make a very large number of runs in a very short time off a very few balls. The Colonel's gamble in putting Bone in to open came off very well that day; he scored sixteen off his first over, a single off the last ball and confronted Ian Bentley whose first delivery to him came down the pitch like a shell and which, his mighty biceps hardly contained by the short sleeves of his shirt, he hit with an ear-splitting crack to disappear amongst the branches of a boundary chestnut tree, much to the astonishment and fluttering indignation of four pigeons who had been roosting in the sunshine. It took some time to find the ball.

Ian Bentley's next delivery seemed to be a repeat of the former ball but it must have been subtly different for, although Bone played exactly the same shot, it bowled him. Nevertheless, our strike rate was better than Windlesham's had been and we took heart.

The first wicket down was a cheerful gap-toothed, skin headed roofer we had met on the scaffolding while doing the works at Oak Farm. Darryl based his general style on that of Bone and – give a few years – it seemed probable that he would one day come to match him in physique. While the Colonel plodded at one end, he swung away at the other connecting to good effect from time to time. How Darryl survived I do not know as ball after ball seemed to miss the stumps by little more than the usually quoted coat of varnish but he made some notable strikes and the Colonel plodded happily on at the other end.

Luck gave out in the end and Darryl was well caught out in the deep. Byam settled a pretty flashy cap (Harlequins, I think) on his head, kissed Gentian on the cheek, patted Claire on the shoulder and set off for the wicket to a chant of "'ere we go, 'ere we go, 'ere we go" from the group of rude little boys who were operating the score board and who were pretty impressed by Byam's general turnout and who obviously expected great things.

They weren't disappointed. Byam stepped well forward to the pitch of the ball and produced one of the sweetest cover drives ever seen, to the rapturous applause of his fan club, female and mature, juvenile and male. It was a good curtain raiser to a good performance and I had to admit that Byam was a cricketer. He took no risks and to my unspeakable joy he carted Bentley all over the place. Runs accumulated. However, Nemesis stalked. Byam had sparkled his way to 42 and the Colonel had crept his way to 32 when the slow bowler with whom Ian Bentley had reluctantly replaced himself, finding that he was incapable of making any impression on the deliberate Colonel and was treated with no respect at all by Byam, sent down a slow long hop. The Colonel opened his ancient shoulders and on drove it with considerable force calling Byam for a run.

As sometimes happens, once or twice in a season I suppose, the ball hit the stumps at the far end and, as hardly ever happens, stopped dead. Ian Bentley, fielding at mid-off, fell on it and put the wicket down. The Colonel and Byam hadn't crossed. Byam was run out with the score at 117 for 3 . The Colonel was mortified. He was horrified. His apologies to Byam, turned lightly aside, were continuous and his misery was compounded by Ian Bentley calling to him for all to hear,

"Thanks Colonel! That'll save us a ball or two!"

And to crown our woes, the next batsman only survived one ball. It had to be confessed that the situation was serious and the chances of the Bentley Cup remaining in Little Hampden were diminishing by the minute and I had so happily seen it in imagination on the Colonel's sideboard. The shadows lengthened across the pitch, the church clock struck five and a grim struggle ensued. Runs mounted slowly, the wickets fell. The Colonel smote on and his score rose with that of the team to 130 for 7 and to 140 and the Colonel was joined by his son-in-law whose only claim to be in the team was that he had once played hockey for the minor counties against Scotland.

Afterwards we decided that his technique was to close his eyes and play a hockey shot. The Colonel's groan every time he did this was audible in the pavilion but so also was the grinding of Ian Bentley's teeth when he connected which he did a surprising number of times. It wasn't a very long episode but it was an extremely fruitful episode – 170 for 8 and it really looked as though we might make it.

Without noticing what she was doing, Iris reached out and held my hand every time Tom faced the bowling. Gentian, who, as she afterwards said, had not smoked since she left school, extracted a Gauloise and a lighter from my jacket and Claire, turning her back on the proceedings, went to help with the washing up. "I couldn't bear the strain," she said afterwards.

The clock struck six and then the half hour. The umpires conferred for a brief moment as to the light but play proceeded. The last man before myself joined the Colonel and they had an earnest conversation during which Tom had instructed him to leave the batting to him.

The field closed in. Ian Bentley resumed the bowling. The wretched tenth man stonewalled valiantly, took a wild swipe at a ball outside the off stump, got an edge which fell just short of second slip. In desperation off the last ball of the over, he swung wildly and he and the Colonel, belting up and down the pitch ran two. 172 for 9. The Colonel resumed the batting, not daring to score a single, desperately anxious to score, repeatedly looking at his watch until

Bentley, who by now was bowling from both ends, sent down amidst his close packed field a nice long hop well outside the leg stump. The Colonel smote it with all his diminishing force and it rattled cheerfully against the pavilion rails. 176 for 9.

"Over!" called the umpire and Bentley hurried down the other end ready to devour our quaking tenth man. Bentley took his usual run, delivered a ferocious ball, knocked the wretched man's leg stump out of the ground. I don't think he had even raised his bat.

The Little Hampden C.C. boasts three pairs of pads. The Colonel was wearing one, the tenth man was wearing the second and to me had fallen the remaining two which were by no means a pair. Claire, dishcloth in hand, tumbled down the pavilion steps. Iris and Gentian, cooing encouragement pushed me forward into the fray. I'm not familiar with Wagnerian opera but I'm sure there must be an appropriate scene – Siegfried being sent into battle by the Valkyrie or would it be against the Valkyrie? Or would it be sent into battle by the Rhine Maidens against the Nibelung? I felt that the thunder of a full orchestra should have accompanied my progress and the operatic and doom-laden atmosphere was sharpened by the dust motes dancing in the rays of the down sloping sun which turned the chestnut trees to gold.

I hope I looked nonchalant. I feared that the strap of one of my pads had come undone or was it the lace of one of my trainers? It was hard to tell. I advanced to the crease, now dusty with the scraping of many nailed boots. In a voice which I had intended should be light and pleasant, but was in fact, I think, plaintive and squeaky, I asked for middle and leg.

Ian Bentley disappeared to the far boundary, turned about, pawed the ground for a moment or two and thundered towards me, his face contorted with rage and hatred, his eyes, I do believe, glowing like lasers. I didn't see the ball he delivered. I heard it. It went past my ear with a whirr like a driven grouse. The second ball was almost identical but at the third ball I really thought the time had come to assert my manhood or perish in the attempt. It was short; it rose like a rocket. I brandished my bat at it. I just got a touch. The ball rose vertically about twenty feet in the air and descended into the confident waiting hands at backward point. He dropped it!

"Fucking Hell!" said Churchwarden Bentley, his sanctimonious public image shattered for a moment.

The Colonel and I strolled to meet each other. "Christ, Jack!" he muttered, "Never ever do that again!"

"I won't!" I said fervently, "I won't!"

"Well," he said as he returned to his crease, "if we don't win now, we don't deserve to win."

The fourth ball was a straight, deadly accurate half-volley, the sort of ball with which I had never succeeded in connecting in my life. I closed my eyes and presented a dead bat to it. It hit me smartly on the thumb.

"How's that?" screamed the demented Mr. Bentley, but the umpire – a good citizen of Little Hampden – disdained even to reply. The fifth ball, slightly outside the leg stump hit me squarely on the elbow and, in a sea of pain, I saw Ian Bentley looking me up and down as one deciding where to strike next.

The ball, when it came, seemed, as the saying used to be, to have my name on it. It hit a bare patch, screamed towards me like a sidewinder missile. In desperation, I flung my bat up to protect myself and was rewarded by a satisfying click. All turned to watch the ball as it rose to an almost incredible height and come to fall with an echoing metallic crash on the roof of the pavilion whence it trickled down to the gutter and fell with a splash in the middle of a large and calorie rich cake covered with butter icing from which, by a freak of ballistics, a glace cherry was propelled through the window of the scoring box. 183 – a tie at the worst!

"Over!" called the umpire.

Bentley, his chest rising and falling with a hoarse choking sound, changed ends and bore down upon the Colonel but the spirit of that Ensign Lindsay Ross who had carried the colours of the Seventy Third Foot through the three days of Waterloo still pulsed in the Colonel's veins. The ball was a good one but the shot was better. With stunning military precision, the Colonel played a nice forward shot. Bentley dived desperately to field it. It eluded his fingers and the Colonel and I ambled gently past each other to score the winning single.

Totally depraved by witnessing similar spectacles on the telly, the youth of Hampden poured onto the pitch. The cricket team of Hampden followed them and formed a cheering avenue for the Colonel.

"Goodness knows," said Iris, "what price I'm going to have to pay for this afternoon! I'll be rubbing his back for a fortnight!"

The teapots had gone but a surprising number of beer crates had taken their place and ranks of plastic beakers stood ready on the tables.

Ian Bentley hurried to his car without a word, but, when he got there, Byam was at hand to open the door for him with exquisite politeness, saying as he did so,

"Your sloppy approach may have been acceptable forty years ago, Bentley, but now we expect something a bit more professional." Bentley, his face contorted with a rage that was scarcely human, sped away and disappeared down the dusty lane.

Iris produced the Bentley Cup and put it on the table. We filled it to the brim and passed it round. The Windlesham team, the animosities of the afternoon forgotten, joined us. Bone produced a bottle of scotch, swearing that he had it on good authority that, taken internally, it was the very best possible thing for bruises. Bemused with triumph, I accepted the plastic beakerful that he offered me.

With twenty two men and probably three times that number of spectators, the beer did not last long and I think it was Tom who suggested that we adjourn to the Sorrel Horse. We did. Somebody put a pint of bitter in my hand. Claire came and sat on my lap and plonked a sticky kiss on my cheek. The tea ladies cheered and my last memory was of Gentian arm in arm with Bone and Darryl, her Benenden voice upraised in a song of which the chorus appeared to be -

"It was a pair of red plush breeches
That kept John Thomas warm."

Chapter Sixteen

The Racing Uncertainty.

"Do you think Byam *really* thinks I look like a golliwog?" said Claire, disconsolately looking at herself in the glass.

"No, certainly not. Well, when you've just washed your hair perhaps."

She continued to survey herself doubtfully. "I expect he thinks I look an awful mess..."

"I can't imagine why you should think so. You look wonderful."

"Oh, you always say that... but when you look at Gentian..."

"Look at Gentian? I never look at Gentian. At least I haven't looked at Gentian since the cricket match."

"Well, I do. Or rather I have. This morning. She dropped in for coffee. The clothes! The hair! The chunky jewellery! She made me feel like a right little wife! Would it be better if I had my hair short, do you think? Or put it up – like this?"

"That's nice, but the question is, would it stay up?"

"Probably not."

"Now, Claire, you look wonderful, and anyway, if faced with a choice between a shetland pony and a bicycle – I'd choose the shetland pony every time."

"Perhaps she is a bit skinny ..."

"Distinctly skinny!"

"She's nice though. She and Byam seem to be getting on like a house on fire but the trouble is Father Woodruffe still can't be brought to approve of Byam."

"So what? Does it matter? They're both old enough to take care of themselves. And does anybody these days really pay attention to what parents think? I didn't ask your old pa whether I could marry *you*... Don't you remember? We just rang him up and told him we were getting married Saturday fortnight at the Bow registry office and we'd love to see him there if he could manage it. That's the right way to do these things." The whole idea of Byam and his doings made me come over all off-hand and aggressively working class sometimes. "So what's so special about old Woodruffe? I can't see why they just don't get on with it and stop making all this fuss!"

"Well if you mean what you usually mean by 'it', I don't think that's the problem. They've been getting on with 'it' very successfully for some time now. And anyway, the difference between my Dad and Gentian's is that my Dad has a teacher's pension, a semi in Acton and a loving heart and Gentian's has several millions, a large estate in Cambridgeshire and a heart of stone!

"Another problem is that there is a bloke hanging around called Robeson-Wathen with whom Gentian had a swing around a few years ago and who, you might say, carries the stable money. She thinks now that he's an awful twit but Daddy Woodruffe is still very impressed by his hyphened surname and his well paid job in the City and obviously considers him a much more suitable parti for Gentian than poor old Byam. Gentian is quite convinced that she'll have her very generous allowance cut if Daddy W. doesn't approve of her intended."

"Approve of her intended? Claire, what are you talking about? It sounds as though you're trying out one of your plots for a Pills and Swoon novel! People don't get cut off without a penny these days for marrying the wrong chap, especially not spoilt daddy's darlings like Gentian!"

I'd heard quite enough about Byam's love life and its problems but my flagging interest was revived by Claire's next pronouncement -

"She had an absolutely dotty idea when she was here this morning but it could just work and you've got to help! Did you know that Father Woodruffe, with a couple of mates, is going to build a racing stables? At Pitt House – that's where they live, just north of Cambridge. Now, we thought, er... Gentian thought, wouldn't it be wonderful if he took on Byam as his architect and Byam made a great success of it? He might even get taken on as the old man's partner if he played his cards right. Who knows? Is that such a dotty idea? Could *we* work it?"

This was beginning to make sense but I was certainly not going to join in a conspiracy to elevate Byam to an undeserved fortune.

"I would think not a hope!" I was able to reply firmly and with some satisfaction.

"Why not?"

"It's already fixed. They've got a mob of tremendously grand American architects on the payroll as far as I've heard."

But, as it happened and in the funny way these things have of turning out, it wasn't such a dotty idea after all ...

One of the members of Woodruffe's consortium dropped out and, by chance, whom should he meet when racing at Newmarket but our old friend Clive Belton. The friendship flourished. They all went rolling back to Moat House, Medfield where, as we gathered, they were extremely impressed by the elegance of the appointments, doubtless beguiled by Little Hermione's hospitality and they finally put the question, "Who was your architect?"

Not above dropping a title or two around if he could, Clive Belton attributed the works to Sir Hastings Munro.

A few days after this encounter, Sir Hastings came into the office, a letter in hand -

"Got a letter here from some builder chappie. Wants to build some stabling at a place called Pitt House somewhere between Newmarket and Ely. Can't think why! I was brought up with horses and I'll tell you – never met a horse in me life that wasn't bloody stupid! Can't think why people want to have anything to do with 'em, but there it is! Might as well go and have a look, I suppose, but I dunno... It seems they've got a scheme from some American outfit. Not too keen on picking up someone else's pieces for them. What do you think?"

"What's this bloke's name?"

"Woodley or something," said Sir Hastings vaguely.

"Wouldn't be Woodruffe, would it?"

"That's right, Woodruffe. What are you doing on Thursday? Go over and take a look, shall we?" and without more ado he picked up the telephone and with cheerful insouciance made an appointment for us to go and call on Woodruffe and his associates.

"You'd better go instead of me," I said later to Byam. "Sir H. won't remember which of us he made the arrangement with.

But in the end, it was decided that we should both go. Sir Hastings, quite unmoved by this augmentation to the party and looking on the outing as a day in the country as much as anything else, made no demur and we set off together.

We stepped out of the car at Pitt House and Sir Hastings stood for a moment, surveying its late Georgian front.

"Know the house well," he said. "Used to come here often when I was a boy. Used to belong to some people called Manton. Mad you know! All quite mad! And Jimmy Manton (the last of 'em) was the worst of the lot! Used to dress in full evening dress every night... high heels, make up, diamond tiara, the lot... dotty as a door-knocker! And now it belongs to this builder fellow... ah, well..."

I did hope that Dennis Woodruffe who had appeared at the top of the steps during the course of Sir Hastings' rumination hadn't heard this slighting reference. Sir Hastings trotted jauntily up the steps.

"Ah, my dear Woodruffe," he said extending a cordial hand. "Sorry we're a little late. Such a nice day, I thought we'd go round by Baldington. So pretty across the water meadows, with the willows just beginning to come out."

I could see that Dennis Woodruffe didn't think this an adequate reason for keeping important people waiting as we had done for over twenty minutes but Sir Hastings continued, unabashed, "Knew you wouldn't mind if I brought two of my fellows with me," and, leading me forward, "This is Alexander," and, waving a hand towards Byam, "And Simpson."

Dennis Woodruffe offered me a limp hand and eyed Byam intently. "Haven't I seen you somewhere before?" he asked.

I didn't think much of the fawning and servile smile, the rictus baring of the teeth which Byam returned this greeting and I thought nothing at all of his reply,

"I'm a friend of your daughter," said Byam. "You lent me a fiver last time we met," he added with an unnecessarily matey laugh.

I didn't think we were making a very good impression and I don't think Dennis Woodruffe did either for he led us without a word into the dining room where three men were sitting round a table covered with papers. Introductions were rapidly made.

"Mr. Belton you know, of course. My associate Mr. Custer and my assistant Mr. Parker." He glanced at his watch reprovingly and resumed, "Well, better get down to it. Parker – give out the papers. Here are the articles of association between me and my colleagues and, as you will see, we formed a consortium called 'Pitt House Ltd.' The intention is, as you will have understood from my letter, to build racing stables here. We have outline planning consent. The scheme exists in draft; it was prepared for us by Heinz and Colville. You've probably heard of them. In Saratoga? I think they're considered to be the leaders in this field and we're certainly satisfied with what they've done so far.

"Approximate costings which my chaps have worked out are on a separate sheet," and testily, to Sir Hastings, "No, that's the schedule of accommodation. No... the blue paper... yes, that's right."

Three large and very glossy A3 brochures were produced and placed in front of us and we studied them in silence for a minute or two, my mind a total blank and hoping that someone on our side would think of something sensible and intelligent to say. I needn't have worried.

Sir Hastings, with a running burble of comment,

"Wonderful people! I spent ten months in the States last year, did you know? Wonderful people! Most ingenious. We can't teach them anything about packaging! Well, well... this is all very useful and interesting. Hmm... entrance off the main road. Wonder if that's the right way to do it? Ground falls to the south? (Got to think about the distant views, y'know!) Remember what Ruskin said – 'An ill placed villa can dethrone a dynasty of hills.' If that's true of an ill placed villa, ha, ha, ha, what about an ill placed racing stable, what? One thing you can't change you know is the siting. Still, it's not a bad job, not a bad job at all. Gives us something to work on anyway."

I could see that this disparaging reference to their extremely expensive feasibility study was not going down well. I could see that Sir Hastings' habit of inhaling his coffee with the maximum noise, a habit to which Byam and I had become so accustomed that we no longer noticed it, wasn't going down very well either and Sir Hastings' unspoken thought that 'these Yankee Doodles do very well, very well indeed when you remember that the damn place was only invented 200 years ago,' was so obvious to me that I had an uneasy feeling that it would not be lost on the company. When Sir Hastings – as it appeared – his precarious concentration on the matter in hand almost exhausted, began to doodle and sketch idly on the pad in front of him, the thought came to me again that we were not making a very good showing, but, rack my brains as I might, I could not think of a thing to say.

It didn't matter. To my astonishment, Byam moved swiftly into gear,

"Heinz and Colville? Yes, this scheme's based on their buildings at Middleton in Texas. It was illustrated in the Architectural Review a year or two ago. There's an article in 'The Field'. I expect you saw it? Certain amount of criticism about the eaves height... I understand they had to pretty well reorganise from scratch the arrangements for the bulk storage of feed. I know this is only preliminary stuff but the insulation looks to me as though it were designed for mid-summer in Texas and not for mid-November in Cambridge, (Cambridge U.K. that is)."

"Now where on earth did he get all this from?" I wondered. "He doesn't know anything about stabling! He's never been to the States in his life! He may have read the odd Dick Francis, but he doesn't know anything about racing either." It wasn't until we got home that I discovered that Gentian had sent Byam copies of every single document on the table in front of us and had rung various influential friends in the States and had obtained copies of magazine articles. Byam's imagination had done the rest.

Dennis Woodruffe began to splutter and so did Mr. Custer. Clive Belton began to look rather self satisfied.

"So what are you saying, Mr. Alexander?" he asked.

"I'm saying," replied Byam crisply, "that your schedule of accommodation is extremely useful to us but the scheme as it stands will need checking – very careful checking."

We batted the matter back and forth for quite a long time. I took – or affected to take notes. It began to emerge that where we were Clive Belton's nominee, Heinz and Colville had been Mr. Custer's nominee. "Forty, fifteen," I thought, "Belton serving."

At the end of this at times heated discussion, Dennis Woodruffe looked at his watch and said, "I don't want to spend too much time on this, though, of course, we note what you say, and perhaps you'll put it in a memo to me, but we've got to be up and racing one year from now and," – rounding on Sir Hastings – "you don't say much, Sir Hastings. Can you give us a bit of your time?"

"Time!" said Sir Hastings. "Right, yes. Do you know what the great Duke of Wellington said? He said, 'Time spent in reconnaissance is never wasted'. The process of design is something you should never rush. I'm always saying that to these fellows. You've got to think of the thing in the round you know. Buildings are three dimensional – I sometimes think buildings are *four* dimensional, talking of time. You've got to get it right! Now you musn't think I don't admire this scheme that's been prepared, but if you want my honest opinion, it's all cover and no contents, ha, ha, ha! What's the phrase people use? All medium and no message. Know what I mean?"

He began to tear sheets from the pad in front of him and scatter them round the table, muttering as he did so,

"Got to think of the approach. The approach comes first, of course. Not too keen on this idea of coming in off the main road. What's wrong with a slip road? Going to be a lot of big vehicles coming and going. Want somewhere to park them, don't want to see nothing but horseboxes, what? Want to see something of the building. This little sketch of theirs, (clever, oh yes, clever) – know what Frank Lloyd Wright said -'Architecture should comfort the human spirit.' Good phrase that, I always thought, good phrase! Good architect, if it comes to that. Now ask yourself, my dear Woodbridge, does this little sketch comfort the human spirit? And what about the equine spirit? Tell me that! No, I think you want to move the entrance onto the slip road... The courtyard should be a great deal wider – no reason in the world why these wings shouldn't terminate with little pavilions. I think of Ledoux – good architect, designed all the gates to Paris, you know. His work has been terribly neglected.

"Now – this is how it ought to be. You're looking down the main entrance. We keep all the vehicles away round this side. You can get straight up onto the gallops, crossing the main road *here* – much safer. Young Simpson was quite right – bulk storage arrangements are pitiful, quite pitiful! No wonder they had to alter them."

Drawing after drawing began to flow across the table, all contrived in the blackest of black inks on seemingly hand made grey paper with a broad-nibbed fountain pen.

"Bloody old magician!" I thought enviously and resentfully. "How the Hell did he do it? Good theatre, though!"

One of Sir Hastings' sketches came to rest in front of me. A string of little horses were walking out between two rusticated pavilions very much in the manner of Ledoux. A low shaft of sunshine from beneath a cloudy sky cast a deep shadow under the eaves. The wind was clearly blowing from the west, leaves streaming away from a bent tree in the foreground set the scene in the autumn and a clump of cow parsley withering away at its foot underlined this impression.

The meeting was undoubtedly extremely impressed.

"Haw, haw, haw," said Sir Hastings. "That's the way to do it! Think three dimensionally, my dear Woodbridge. Don't want anyone at the end of the day to say it could have just as well been done with a Lego set, what? Ha, ha, ha!"

"Get these printed, Parker! Ask them to put some sandwiches up. Find out what everybody wants to drink!" said Dennis Woodruffe.

When we got home Sir Hastings wandered off into the private side of the house, saying as he did so, "Well, get something worked up on those lines, would you?" and it was clear to us that he thought he had done all that he was called upon to do. As a matter of fact, as time went by, it became fairly clear that he was right in that his scheme worked, with only minor modifications, extremely well and Byam and Ron set out to deal with it.

I rather lost touch at this juncture because, unexpectedly, I found myself involved with another member of the racing fraternity, this time – and most inconveniently – near Newbury on the Berkshire Downs. The client in the case was none other than Brigadier Molyneux and his reason for coming to us was simple: both he and his exalted patron had been extremely impressed by 'The Prince of Wales'. Two unexpected things had happened in the Brigadier's life. Firstly, he had had a surprise offer for his own racing establishment and secondly, he had just inherited a handsome but extremely delapidated house. Time was obviously of the essence and he needed to vacate his own house within a very few months and needed to make his new house habitable.

At first, I was very dubious about this; Newbury is a very long way indeed from Lavenham and at first I agreed only to "go and have a look". One thing led to another and soon I found myself involved in the restoration of a substantial 17th Century house and, as I say, lost touch with Dennis Woodruffe and the dealings of Pitt House Ltd. Occasionally I looked over Byam's shoulder, occasionally he brought drawings out for my approval, occasionally I gave a piece of advice.

"Have you had any test holes dug?" I asked.

"No – I suggested it – " and then with a very plausible imitation of Dennis Woodruffe, "Test holes? Quite unnecessary! Solid chalk from one end to the other. Dig where you like – it's all the same. You architects! Always wasting time! But this time you can take no for an answer!"

"Get it in writing!" I said.

"That's right," said Ron who'd been listening to this. "Get it in writing."

In the fullness of time Pitt House Stables began to develop on the drawing board, through the local authority and, ultimately, on site. The consortium quarrelled among themselves. Twice Byam called Sir Hastings to his aid to defend a design aspect of the scheme.

"It's not so much Woodruffe," he said, "who only wants one thing and that is to get the job started on site. And finished. It's not so much Clive Belton who's really as good as gold. It's that bloody Custer! He and Woodruffe are at loggerheads the whole time and perpetually manoeuvring to get Clive Belton on their side. It's very wearing I can tell you! I only hope they can stay together long enough for us to get the bloody thing built! Of course, they've all got each other by the balls really because, under the terms of their agreement, any one of them can withdraw at any time and the other two are obliged to buy him out. Custer's the only one who knows the first thing about racing, Woodruffe's the only one who knows the first thing about building. You'd think I was the only one who knew the first thing about architecture and so it is but they won't accept it! So, what with Custer changing every bloody thing I specify, Woodruffe ringing up every five minutes of the day to ask why this that or the other hasn't been done, I've lost about half a stone."

"But what about Gentian? How's that all going?"

"Oh, wonderful!" said Byam, swallowing convulsively, a glazed look coming over his eyes. "She's wonderful! I don't know where we'd be without her! She's always ringing me up and marking my card – giving me all the winners you might say. If there's a storm coming up she warns me. I can't tell you how useful it is. Gives me time to get my act together. Wouldn't like to be doing this without good old Gentian!"

"And what about Daddy Woodruffe? Is he coming round? Does he think you're going to train on as he might put it?"

"Well, if I've just given him the wherewithal to frustrate Custer, yes, but if I've been forced to give Custer the wherewithal to frustrate him, no."

"What about the cost of works? Is that under control?"

"Oh, that's really rather up to Woodruffe and his in-house quantity surveyors. Doesn't seem to be too bad but it's getting very near the edge. Tremendous debate last week, for example – ought we to reduce this and ought we to reduce that? I stood out for the scheme, of course, the whole scheme and nothing but the scheme and thus made an enemy of Custer and finally pulled out and left the two of them at it hammer and tongs on the subject of the cost of works. Still, they'll have to pipe down soon – we start on site next week."

"All tooled up are you?"

"More or less," said Byam dubiously, "More or less."

Claire and I went down to Newbury for that weekend and we returned to find that a considerable drama had developed. In our short absence the ground had opened under Byam's feet. Literally.

Chapter Seventeen

The Racing Uncertainty (contd.)

Woodruffe Construction had taken possession of the site and heavy earth-moving equipment in surprising numbers began to crawl backwards and forwards over Pitt Meadow. On the first morning of the contract one of the diggers hit a soft spot, reported this to the site agent, skirted round it and carried on. A very few minutes later, they hit another one and, a few minutes after that, a third.

Further investigations revealed a similarity between all the holes. They were circular and about twenty feet in diameter. The soil was reasonably well compacted but this was undoubtedly made-up ground and one of them was found to be full, not very far below the surface, of timbers, bricks, tiles and other objects of considerable age.

While we were down in Newbury Byam had been doing a good deal of running backwards and forwards and finally gave instructions for one of these strange pits to be dug out. It was about thirty feet deep and the walls were solid chalk. The site was indeed solid chalk, as Dennis had said, from end to end but he had reckoned without the pits.

As soon as we got back from Berkshire, Byam hurried round to tell us all about it.

"It's a bugger," he said, "I don't know what we're going to do! Haven't broken the news to Woodruffe yet – he's been away too, thank goodness! – He's not going to like it! I wish I knew what on earth they were! And why didn't he know they were right there on his land? We'll have to pile all the foundations down that end of the site. It's going to cost the earth!"

"How much of the site is affected?" I asked.

"The whole of the west block, practically the whole of the living quarters, probably the little bridge over the slip road (I'm not quite sure about that). Why don't you come down and have a look at it tomorrow? I've never seen anything like it!"

The next day we stood side by side, peering down into the first of Byam's pits. The sides were, indeed, solid chalk and the bottom of the pit was solid chalk likewise.

As Byam and I grumbled, cursed and wondered, peevishly throwing stones into the hole, I heard Claire squeak and then fall silent, pointing like a spaniel.

"Let's go down and have a look. I think I might know just what this is or was... Get that ladder..."

Minutes later, she stood at the bottom of the pit. She looked very small down there.

"Hey, Miss!" shouted the site agent, "Hard hat area! Can you catch?" and he threw his hat down to her.

I followed her down. The atmosphere was strange, cold and clammy and, I thought, pretty spooky. Large eyed and wondering, Claire looked round her and up at the encircling wall. She paused for a moment, then moved over to the wall of the pit and kicked at a patch of earth which fell inwards and revealed a tiny tunnel.

"Thought so," she said, "It's a Neolithic flint mine! It's just like Grimes Graves. This is one of the lateral shafts and I'll bet there are others. Look, there's one up there."

"Grimes Graves?" said Byam. "Good God... you're right! Flint mine!

"Archaeological discovery of some moment!" I said.

"Christ!" said Byam as the significance of this dawned on him. "What shall we do? Fill it in quick? We can't! Lord, Dennis is going to love this! Know what we've got here? A registered Ancient Monument... £1.50 a time and reduced rates for school groups. At least it's not registered yet but it very soon will be. Now I come to think of it... you know what this field's called? It's called Pitt Meadow on the old estate maps. Now we know why!"

"Pitt Meadow! Of course! Ought we to have known about this?" asked Claire.

"Dennis told you not to bother about test holes, didn't he? Did you get that in writing?"

"No," said Byam, "I'm pretty sure... no, dammit! I didn't! I missed the chance at the time. Often thought about it later but there never seemed to be the right moment. You know how it sometimes is."

I knew how it sometimes was.

We climbed the ladder and sat, our legs dangling, on the edge of the pit but very soon the rising cold drove us away and we were very glad to accept the offer of a cup of tea in the site agent's office.

"When's Dennis Woodruffe back?" I asked.

"On Thursday," said Byam.

"He isn't you know!" said the site agent rubbing a clean patch in the dusty window and pointing with his thumb at a striding figure in cap, Barbour jacket and wellingtons, advancing across the site towards us.

Dennis Woodruffe banged his way into the hut. "What in Hell's going on, John?" he snapped to the site agent. "What the devil's that bloody great heap of spoil down the bottom of the site? Whose authority was it? Oh, good afternoon, Mr. Alexander. What have you got to tell me about all this? Who gave instructions for those pits to be dug?"

"Well," said the site agent, quite unabashed and clearly determined not to be given the run-around by Woodruffe, "well, if we're to believe Mrs. Simpson's theory, the answer is – it was Neolithic Man!"

"Neolithic Man? What the Hell do you mean? And who's Mrs. Simpson?"

Introductions were made (to which Woodruffe paid scant attention) and we explained our theory; we described Grimes Graves to him; we explained the Neolithic flint mining system as best we could remember it and took him to see the hole. He became extremely subdued.

"Are there any more of these things?" he asked the site agent. "Not as far as you know? Well we must get the engineers onto this. Tomorrow at the latest. We'll have to pile all the foundations at this end of the site. It's not going to be cheap!" And to Byam, "Couldn't this have been anticipated?"

"Yes," said Byam, "it could have been anticipated. Test holes would have uncovered these."

Woodruffe bit his lip, glared at Byam for a minute, then with an effort, "You suggested it. It's all right. I haven't forgotten. I was the bloody fool who said don't bother. Come outside a minute."

And we watched him and Byam walk slowly away across the site, their heads together.

Claire and I went back to the car.

"What do you suppose they're talking about?"

"I know very well what they're talking about! They're just wondering how they're going to sell this to the ever enchanting Mr. Custer."

"How serious is it?"

"It would be quite serious enough if they had to pile this end of the site. Woodruffe's right. It would cost a bomb. But when the archaeologists get hold of this and, obviously, they will get hold of it, I doubt if they'll be allowed to build on this end of the site at all. In fact, I'm absolutely certain that they won't. You don't find a Neolithic flint mine every day! And look at the tourist attraction that Grimes Graves has become!"

"My father told me that when he was a boy," Claire said excitedly, "there was nobody there at all. He was evacuated to Norfolk in the war and he and his mates used to play around in that area – he got to know them very well. There was just a rickety ladder down into the pit and you could crawl as far as you liked down the shafts. Used to give me the creeps when he talked about it! Fascinating though!"

"Well?" we both enquired anxiously when Byam returned.

"Sorry to take so long," he said, settling into the driving seat. "It took me quite a long time to persuade him that he should forget any thought of building on this end of the site. It mightn't be the end of the world. They'd have to fill in all the excavation they've done beyond block B and they'd have to extend A and C and resite block

B in what used to be the middle of the courtyard. Means moving the whole thing up the site and brings it uncomfortably close to the road but, if the planners will wear it, I think it could be done. It's going to be a damn site cheaper than any other possible way out. There'll be a helluva delay while we get this sorted... "

"And what did he say to all that?"

"He's no fool once you get the idea into his head. No fool at all. He saw the point. Of course we can't hush it up and of course we'll have to ring the County Archaeologist and of course, we'll just have to let it rip. It's newsworthy though... TV cameras, unclimbable fence all the way round the site. Not good news, however you look at it."

"Wouldn't suit Woodruffe to have a money-spinning tourist attraction on his estate, I suppose?"

"Absolutely not! But that's not the point. You know what a lot of trouble he's had with Custer? Well he thinks Custer will pull out and might mount an action for damages for negligence."

"Negligence? Whose negligence?" I was beginning to get rather uneasy, not quite liking Byam's icy calm.

"Mine, yours, Sir Hastings', ours..."

"But for God's sake! He lost no time at all in admitting that the negligence was his."

"I rather liked him for that," said Claire.

"Yes, that's right," said Byam, "but it's one thing to admit to negligence to you and me and Claire but it's quite another to admit it to your partners. They all have to bear a share of the loss you know. They'll be looking round for somebody to blame."

"Better for us if Custer did bail out."

"It would sink the job if he did. Where are they going to pull in the missing capital?"

"How did you leave it?"

Byam drove on for a while in silence before replying. "Look here," he said, "let's not lose sight of the main chance."

"To begin with – why are we doing this job?"

"Why do we do any job? To earn an honest crust, of course."

"Well, yes, that comes into it."

"Gentian!" said Claire.

"Well, now," said Byam, "this is what we agreed – would we keep quiet about his refusal to sink test holes?"

"Oh dear," said I "we've got to guard our backs at the end of the day."

" 'I'll see you're all right' says he. 'I'll give you that in writing, if you like,' says he. And then some pretty venomous things about Custer. He'd get rid of him tomorrow if it weren't for the capital shortfall."

"Did you agree?"

"Yes."

"Did you ask for an indemnity in writing?"
"No."
"Think he'll run out on you?"
"I don't think so. But, if he does, there were witnesses to his admission."
"Not sure that Jack and I would be considered to be very dispassionate witnesses," said Claire. "What about the site agent?"
"Wouldn't trust it – he's one of Woodruffe's men. Might have gone a bit deaf, you know."
"It's a bit dodgy," I said.
"Well what would you have done?"
"Same as you, I expect. Can you trust him not to do a runner on you?"
"Got to. Got to."
That night and just as we were rolling into bed, Claire summed up the day's doings-
"So let's get this straight. In order to ingratiate himself with old Woodruffe, gallant Byam offers himself as a sacrifice."
"No, not gallant Byam! Bloody inefficient, selfish Byam!" I yelled, my anger finally breaking. "And it'll not be Byam but poor old Sir Hastings who is put on the altar."
"Well, yes, that's about it... Yes, of course, you're right. What a mess! Has Sir H. got um... negligence... um... what's it called?"
"Professional indemnity insurance. Yes, of course he has. I filled in the form for him myself, oh, about three months ago, beginning of January, when the insurance company sent the reminder round. Gave it to Heather to get the old bird to sign it and send off the first premium. I filled it out for a million pounds worth of cover. Thought I'd overestimated perhaps but now... well we could find ourselves having to cough up that sort of money, I'm afraid."
"Ouf! That' s a relief then! Clever Jack!"
"Yes. Yes. I'm glad that's taken care of."

After a sleepless night I tore off to Spring House at first light and was not surprised to see Byam bounding up the steps as I inserted my key.
He grinned nervously, "I expect we're both on the same mission?"
"Ransacking Sir Hasting's files?"
"That's about it. Just thought we ought to check on that insurance certificate. I remember we discussed the amount we ought to write down for cover. I suggested 2 million but you thought 1 million was enough. Hope you were right, Jack."
We made our way into Heather's office and were standing about not quite certain where to start looking, peering at the labels on the front of the filing cabinets and started like naughty schoolboys on hearing a racking cough behind us.

"Can I help you gentlemen?" asked Heather suspiciously.

"You certainly can, Heather old love," smarmed Byam, moving swiftly into gear. "Look, you wouldn't happen by chance to know where the Professional Indemnity Certificate is kept would you?"

"Yes, I would happen and not by chance either! I do have a filing system you know. If you look between O and Q you may find something beginning with P." She sniffed smugly.

We pulled out the drawer marked M-S and, sure enough, nestling between Organs and Quinquennials we found a red paper wallet marked Professional Indemnity Insurance. Steadying my hand, I opened it and drew out the thin contents.

The top sheet bore my handwriting and was the form I remembered filling in. I opened it, looking eagerly for the familiar, florid, thick black and all-important signature. No signature. Just a blank. And a little yellow stick-on note in Sir Hastings' hand saying – 'Heather – can't see the point of this can you? H.M.'

"Could you Heather?" asked Byam.

"Could I what?"

"Could you see the point?"

"Certainly not! Waste of money! Would have cost us ten thousand pounds a year. Lot of nonsense! We've never needed one. At least, not till you came!"

"Heather," said Byam, "you're making me very unhappy!"

Chapter Eighteen

Women and Horses.

Because it was very difficult to get Sir Hastings to listen to anything that was being said and because, even when his attention had been engaged, it was easily diverted and because he gave a very great deal more of his time to the writing of his book than to the professional affairs of the firm, it was easy to forget what a very good architect he was.

He had been born with every advantage into an influential and wealthy family and he had married a good deal of money as well. He started in practice just as wartime austerities were beginnimng to melt away and at a time when such advantages were still advantageous. He had been dealt some good cards but they would have been as nothing if he had not had the skill to play them. He had an extraordinarily perceptive imagination as to how people lived and moved and thought. He had a four dimensional imagination and was able to think not only into the past but also into the future as well and into the here and now. We had been astonished at the fluency with which his Pitt House sketches translated into reality and by the ease with which the detail dropped into place. We had not looked forward to telling him of the problem which had fallen upon us but we needn't have worried.

It never for a moment occurred to him to ask why the problem had not been anticipated. Sparing with his praise, he was incapable of apportioning blame. Such a thing would be way beyond the horizon of his interest. In fact, having grasped the problem and having accepted that his noble scheme required entirely to be redesigned, he set about the task with considerable relish.

"Ha! Ha! Ha!" he said. "Well, now. Let me see. What we've got to accept is that we've got two sites if you follow me – an archaeological site and a building site. This is the archaeological site..." A 6B pencil swept in a graceful double curve across the site. "This bit up here's for Neolithic Man and these are his pits or his pots or whatever you call them. One, two, three. And this is the way into the archaeological site, off the little back road. And here's the office."

"Office?" I said.

"Yes. Office. There'll be scores of people coming to look at the pits. Bound to want an office. Bound to want a shop too. Souvenirs y'know. Papier mâché copies of the Willendorf Venus and all that sort of thing. Bogs too. People can't go anywhere nowadays if they're more than a hundred yards from a bog. (Toilets, they call them. Toilets indeed!)"

He wrote Bogs/Shop on the drawing and continued, "Now as for the rest of the site, all you need to do is to turn Block A through 90 degrees. The little lobby that was at the north end is going to be on the east side – here. Block A will have to move over a bit – no it won't – plenty of room, plenty of room. There you are! See how magnificent it becomes! In many ways, better than it was before!"

"Getting a bit near the main road, perhaps?" asked Byam.

"No," said Sir Hastings firmly. His pencil skittered across the page and a series of little mop-like trees appeared along the boundary. "There you are, you see," he said. "Always a way round these things." And he sauntered nonchalantly away leaving us looking at each other, in Byam's case with vociferous excitement, in my case dumb with admiration and in Ron's case something approximating to proprietorial pride.

The revised scheme, once again, worked as well as its predecessor. Ron, Byam and I erased, drew, traced and adapted and, in an amazingly short time – little more than ten days as I remember – we were back where we had been before the pits opened.

Woodruffe, when Byam presented the scheme to him, was extremely impressed as was also our staunch ally Clive Belton. Custer, on the other hand, was not amused. We only heard about this later and, of course, through the medium of Gentian's impeccable spy system.

"How the Hell did this happen?" Custer had asked, not unreasonably. And, of course, it wasn't long before the absence of test holes was identified as the root cause.

"So," said Custer, summing up, "It's all the fault of that architect of yours, bloody Sir Hector! And that lout Alexander! I knew it wouldn't be long before they put something over on us. But they'll very soon find out that they're trying that on with the wrong man! There's an action for negligence here! Plainest case I ever saw in my life! That Alexander would wriggle himself out of anything – let's see if he can wriggle himself out of this one!"

"Can't sue for negligence unless you can prove damage," said Clive.

"Damage? Of course there's damage – not getting the scheme we agreed."

"Never would have done," said Dennis Woodruffe, "whether the test holes were sunk or not. We just would have found out about it a bit sooner, that's all. Haven't lost anything."

"Time! That's what we've lost – time!"

And then to Woodruffe, "This famous site of yours – supposed to be your contribution – not such a good site after all. Half the size, for one thing. But look here – bring a successful action against these architects, get damages against them, put the money back in the pot, and I might not say anything about the drop in site value... Well? What about it?"

Woodruffe paced the room for a while and finally turned to face the steaming Custer.

"Can't bring an action against the architects. Because why? They suggested that test holes ought to be sunk and I told them not to bother. That's why."

"*You* told them not to bother? They have that in writing? No? Well then! Good God! It's their word against yours!"

The battle, on the evidence of Gentian who had settled herself under the open window, raged backwards and forwards for an hour and more and ended, as might have been anticipated, with Custer roaring away in one direction, to send in his resignation by his solicitor, with Clive driving pensively away in another direction shaken but determined to hang in there and Woodruffe, enraged but exhausted, still slumped in his chair.

"I said to him," said Gentian, "I said to him, 'Daddy, darling – I was proud of you!' And I was! But all the same, they can't replace Custer's capital. Daddy says the work will have to stop in a month because the Bank won't move without another guarantor and Daddy and Belton are fully committed already. Poor old bastard!" she went on, affectionately referring to her father, "Poor old thing! He really looked as though he'd put his foot on the teeth of a rake! I've never seen the poor old poppet so low."

What with the fearful pressure on our already stretched drawing office resources generated by the change in the Pitt House scheme, I had, over the last few weeks, sadly neglected the Brigadier and his Newbury mansion. Indeed, I only woke up to the realities at the very last minute and realised that the contract documents and drawings all neatly bundled and tagged were sitting on my desk on a day when they should, without fail, have been sitting on the Brigadier's desk in distant Newbury.

"No problem at all," said Claire. "I'll drive them down tomorrow. Tomorrow be alright? Perhaps I'll take Gentian with me."

"Gentian?"

"Yes, Gentian. She's longing to see the Brig's house. It seems that some old aunt of her mother's used to live there. I'll give her a ring."

And so it was that Gentian and Claire drove together down to Newbury. We had rung the Brigadier to tell him that his contract drawings would be delivered 'by hand' but I had omitted to say by hand of whom and he was, characteristically and totally delighted to receive Claire and Gentian.

"You know what he's like!" said Claire, "Couldn't take his eyes off Gentian's bum! Took us out and bought us a stupendous lunch. Filled us to the brim with rare wine – at least filled Gentian up with rare wine – old muggins was, of course, driving, and then gave us the royal tour of the stabling."

"Did he sign the contract documents? And did you remember to witness them? And have you brought the counterpart back with you? That was, after all the point of the expedition!" I said testily.

"Yes, yes," said Claire, "Of course we did! And anyway – you say that was the point of the expedition – but I'm not so sure about that! Par exemple – listen to this! When we'd finished the tour, Gentian said something like – 'You're going to bc very sad to give all this up?' And the Brig said yes he would be terribly sad but it had really got too much for him lately. It wasn't so much the racing but the day to day running of a place like that and the endless hassle had begun to get him down and then, 'Don't want to get out of racing altogether – be very glad to buy in as a sleeping partner in some little outfit.' So Gentian said to him, all casual like, 'Are you going to the Cesarewitch on Wednesday and the Brig said yes, he'd got a horse running ... Diadem something... what's it called?.. Snow Diadem! That's it. Not much fancied, I gather, but there you are. And Gentian gave him a dazzling smile and said, 'See you there then, Walter!'"

"Walter?"

"Yes, 'Call me Walter (my friends call me Wally.)' said the Brig over the nuts and wine at the end of our lunch party."

"Wally indeed! Byam and I call him 'Sir'!"

"So after a hug or two and a chaste kiss – at least chaste as far as I was concerned – not quite so chaste as far as Gentian was concerned – we set off for home. Ho for Pitt House where we found Woodruffe not uninterested in the day's events, deciding that, after all, he too would go to the Cesarewitch on Wednesday. I said, 'Invite him back to supper afterwards!' You've got a case of 'Where thou leadest, I will go,' as far as Gentian and the Brig are concerned."

"What did Woodruffe say?"

"Morosely – 'Got another one of those, have we?' But he was pretty impressed. He'd heard of the Brig and – well you never know, do you?"

"Just what the Hell are you supposed to represent?" I said to Byam when he came into the office on Wednesday. Indeed, the checked suit, the discreet felt hat, the race glasses slung casually over the shoulder, (borrowed from a friend for the day as I later discovered), a copy of the Sporting Times in his hand, he presented an image which, amongst so many others, I had not seen before. "Don't tell me – you're going to the Cesarewitch with Gentian, Dennis, Wally – God what a set up! Don't you ever nauseate yourself?"

"Often, often," said Byam equably, adjusting the rake of his hat in the office mirror and to Heather who came in at that moment,

"Would you have me as a son-in-law, Heather, if you saw me coming through the door? How do I look?"

"Very nice," said Heather and it was clear that she thought so.

After this build-up, the out-come was predictable but nontheless satisfactory for that. Snow Diadem, to the surprise of the stable, ran a good third, carrying a substantial place bet at long odds for Heather, to her gratification. The party did indeed adjourn to Pitt House where drawings, finance and horses were discussed over a bottle or two of Madame Clicquot's best and, in a very few days, the Brig slipped comfortably into the slot vacated by Custer who had learned from his solicitor that an action for negligence could hardly lie against anyone.

It only remains to record that, as will be remembered, the winner of the Cesarewitch that year was a long-priced outsider called Wedding Bells.